VAIN

The Complete Series

New York Times & USA Today Bestselling Author
Deborah Bladon

Copyright

First Print Edition, September 2014
Copyright © 2014 by Deborah Bladon
ISBN-13: 978-1502470669
ISBN-10: 1502470667
Cover Design by Wolf & Eagle Media.

Also by Deborah Bladon

The Obsessed Series
The Exposed Series
The Pulse Series

Coming Soon

SOLO

VAIN

PART ONE

Chapter 1

"You're staring at my dick."

I am. I can't even deny it. I guess I can come up with some excuse. Maybe I can pretend to be my best friend, Sadie, and say that I'm studying to be a doctor and I'm doing a thorough, visual exam of his enormous, erect penis. Who answers the door naked? He must have been masturbating. Do people do that? Do they masturbate while they wait for a sandwich to be delivered?

"Sweetheart. Up here." His hand floats past his crotch and my eyes slowly drift along with it, like I'm a fish dangling on a hook.

"What?" My voice isn't my own. I sound all breathy and aroused.

"How much?" He motions towards me and I reel myself back into the reality of the moment. After I finished my dinner with Sadie and her husband, I offered to deliver the sandwich for them when their regular delivery guy went home sick. Knowing the owner of Axel Boston certainly had its perks. I got a free dinner and now this. No tip required at all. Thank you, sir with the naked cock.

"You already paid," I say as I try to keep my gaze focused on his dark brown eyes. The hair on his head almost matches the color of his eyes, which matches the hair that surrounds his…

"No." He walks towards a large round table in the foyer of his apartment. Technically, it's the penthouse since I had to ride the elevator with the doorman and his special key. I wonder what this guy does for a living that affords him the luxury of living here. Maybe he's a porn star. "What's your name, sweetheart?"

"Alexa," I offer. "What's your name?"

He turns quickly as he stops dead in his tracks. I was admiring his perfectly sculpted ass until he turned back around and now I get to stare at his cock again. I might have to take that job delivering sandwiches after all.

"My name is none of your fucking business," he barks at me.

I take a step back when I realize that I've offended him. The fact that I'm practically drooling all over his naked body doesn't bother him at all, but when I ask his name he flips out? I'll just pretend that I can't hear him and use the rest of the time at the door to soak in his body before I go home and tease myself for hours until I…

"How much?" His voice interrupts me yet again and I wonder now if maybe he doesn't understand English.

"I said," I speak loudly and slowly. "You. Already. Paid. For. It."

"Get your pretty little ass in here." He grabs me by my arm and yanks me into his apartment. I turn and stare as the door flies shut behind me.

"I have plans." I tap my black stiletto impatiently on the marble floor. I was supposed to drop off this sandwich and then meet some sorority sisters for a welcome back party. This is only my second night back in Boston after being in Paris for months. I need some good, old-fashioned American fun.

"You're going to bail because of it, aren't you?" He turns and stares right through me. "I'm paying you to fuck me. It's going to be worth it, Alexa."

"What?" I steal one more glance at his cock before I decide that being called a two-bit floozy isn't worth the chance to get fucked by that. "What the hell is your problem?"

"Women like you always bolt when they see it." His voice is deep and low. It bites right through me. "The agency said you'd be fine with it when I requested a blonde."

"I brought you a sandwich." I throw the bag at him and it bounces off his muscular chest before it falls to the marble floor. "Your hooker isn't here yet. I'm not her."

"You brought me a sandwich?" He stares at the crumpled mess on the floor. "I thought you were someone else."

"Obviously," I shoot back as I turn on my heel to leave. "For the record, I wouldn't bolt seeing a cock like that normally."

"I wasn't talking about my dick," he growls.

I pivot back and stare at him. "What then?"

"The scar," he hisses as he tilts his head back. "Women always run when they see the scar."

"What scar?" I've stared at his cock long enough to realize that it's perfect and scar free.

"This scar." His hand jumps to his face before his index finger traces a line down a scar running the length of his cheek.

"Is that why you walk around with your cock flying every which way?" I turn the doorknob in my hand. "It's a good tactic."

"Alexa," he says my name just as I'm stepping over the threshold into the hallway. "Stay."

"Excuse me?" I suck in a tight, fast breath. "I told you I'm not your hooker."

As if on cue, the elevator chimes its arrival. I turn to look, half expecting to see a slut with an over-the-top back-combed blonde wig, blue eye shadow and a leopard print mini skirt stepping off. I'm stunned by the beautiful woman who thanks the doorman before her eyes lock with mine. She's petite, elegantly dressed and her hair is cut into a fashionable blonde bob.

"There are two of you?" The British lilt in her voice makes her that much more attractive. I guess I shouldn't have taken such strong offense at being called a call girl. I thought I looked hot tonight, but next to her I look like a rank amateur. The short black halter dress I have on pales in comparison to the tailored red shift dress she's wearing.

"No." I shake my head a little too vigorously. "I'm not part of this. I'm leaving."

"That's a shame." Her brown eyes run slowly over my body and I realize that she's game for just about anything. I'm not. The only game I want to play tonight involves my battery operated boyfriend and mental images of the naked man she's about to jump into bed with. Three is definitely a crowd for me.

"Wait." His low voice is edged with a plea. "I want to ask you something."

"Are you talking to me or blue eyes?" The beautiful blonde's eyes narrow as she turns towards our naked host. Blue eyes? I've been called a host of things in my life but that's a new one. Given the fact that our body shapes, hair color and height are almost on par, I guess the one distinguishing factor is our eye color. Good on her for noticing a small detail like that when there's a loose cock in the room.

"You can go." He pushes past her and walks out into the hallway to where I'm standing next to the now closed elevator. I have to give the doorman props for not reacting at all when he caught sight of the resident of the penthouse without any clothing. He didn't bat an eyelash as he stood silently watching the doors close before the lift whizzed back down to the lobby. Maybe it's a regular occurrence here. Maybe I need to look for an apartment in this building. The only men I've seen naked in my building are the ones I bring home. I can't say any of them have been as memorable as this man.

"You pay whether or not you play." Her accent has suddenly vanished in wake of his dismissal.

He casts his eyes down at her before he grabs my arm. "Alexa, come back in inside."

"Is that your real name? Are you new?" His scheduled companion for the evening is full of questions that I don't want to answer. "Who do you work for?"

Is she serious? That's the second time tonight I've been mistaken for a prostitute. "I don't…" I trail as I search the air for what should come next. I don't turn tricks? I don't sleep with men for money? I don't know how I ended up talking to a gorgeous naked man and a call girl?

"How much?" he barks at her as he guides me back into his apartment.

"Fifteen hundred and a generous tip is always appreciated." Her perfectly manicured hand dashes out in front of her to wait for the offering.

"A tip?" He rifles through a drawer in the foyer table and pulls out a sizeable wad of cash. "You didn't even strip."

"I can change that," she purrs as she turns in front of me. "Blue eyes, unzip me."

I take a step back. I'm not touching her or her overpriced dress. I reach into my clutch for my smartphone. Maybe if I appear busy these two will keep their bartering to themselves. The only message I have waiting for me is one from Sadie, thanking me again for delivering the sandwich. I should be the one thanking her.

"Keep your clothes on." His voice is thick and measured. "Here's your money."

She gleefully scoops the money into her palm and turns to walk out the still open door of his apartment. "Thanks, baby and for the record, I love tattoos."

Chapter 2

Tattoos. He's covered in them. My eyes have been so focused on his now half erect cock that I haven't given myself a chance to soak in the beauty of the art that covers his chest, back and arms. Each design is intricate, balanced and striking. He's perfect.

"I'm Noah Foster." It's a declaration that catches me off guard.

"I'm Alexa Jackson," I counter even though I know he already knows my first name. I want to hear him say it again. I love the growl that escapes from deep within him when he speaks.

"The Noah Foster." His brow furrows as he stresses the words.

"The Noah Foster?" I repeat unsure if he's trying to sound completely narcissistic or if I'm misinterpreting.

He only nods in response.

"I need to go the Noah Foster." I'll play his game. For this being only my second night back in Boston, it's been one of the most memorable in all my twenty-two years. "I have plans."

"You're not the regular delivery person." He leans back against the door of his apartment, and crosses his muscular arms across his chest. He's impressive and he knows it. He's definitely more than six feet tall. If I had to venture a guess based on the height of my heels, I'd say he's hovering right around the six foot four inch mark. That's almost a full foot taller than me.

The regular delivery person is an elderly man named Bernie. I'd met him months ago when Sadie introduced me to him. "Bernie is sick," I say while I'm trying desperately to keep my eyes fixed to his ridiculously handsome face.

"You're the stand in?" He nods at me. "That's quite the improvement."

I smile slightly at the odd compliment. He doesn't strike me as the type of man who eagerly hands out accolades to just anyone. "I was doing a friend a favor."

"If you don't deliver food, what do you do?" The question comes with a subtle proposition. He's actually interested in what I do? Or maybe he's still hell bent on me being his fuck buddy for the night. Everything about him screams control and expectation.

"I'm a teacher," I say the words with pride. I am a teacher. It's taken me years to accomplish my goal of getting a degree in education. I'm close now. I'm just one semester away from graduating.

"You're a teacher?" His gaze rakes over me lazily. "I don't know another teacher that looks like you."

My eyes float from his face down to his groin and then back up again. "Your loss."

A sly grin pulls at the corner of his mouth. "Let's get to the point."

"The point?" I parrot back. "What point?"

"Do you know who I am?" he asks without any hesitation in his voice at all.

"Yes." I sigh. This guy's confidence is bursting out of every pore in his rock hard body. It's no wonder though. He's what women dream about when they're home alone. "You're the Noah Foster."

His eyes brighten as his full lips part in a broad smile. "You have no idea, do you?"

I feel like the timid mouse in a game of chase with a big, bad, bold cat. "About?" I ask expectantly. He must be somebody beyond a guy who walks around buck naked all the time. Since he hasn't been on one of the Internet gossip sites I frequent a lot, he's a nobody to me. Correction, he's a gorgeous nobody with a ridiculously appealing dick.

"Who I am," he volleys back calmly. "You seriously don't know who I am?"

I take a step back feeling as though I need to make room for his massive ego. "No," I answer firmly. "Who are you?"

He shakes his head slightly before he brushes past me. "Do you have any tattoos, Alexa?" The way he ignores my question pulls on my frustration. I should fish my smartphone back out of my purse and Google him on the spot. Is he a tattoo artist? That would make sense given the beautiful artwork he's proudly displaying all over his ripe, aching-to-be-licked body.

"Tattoos?" I ask. Did that sound as naïve as I think it did? When did I become such a muttering idiot? I've seen naked men before. I've seen men with tattoos before. Why is my brain bouncing around so much? Why can't I seem at least vaguely intelligent right now?

He's directly in front of me now and I can smell the musky combination of his skin and whatever cologne he's slathered all over his body. His eyes drop straight to the top of my breasts. They're pushed so tightly together it's a wonder I can even breathe. "Is any of this beautiful body of yours covered with ink?"

I exhale sharply as his index finger lightly brushes across my neck. "I don't have any of those. No tattoos." I wince inside when I say it. I've never wanted one. What if he thinks that my unmarked body isn't up to par with what he wants? Why the hell do I care?

"Have you modelled?" His warm breath skirts over my skin as he leans even closer. It's taking every ounce of willpower I have not to reach out to grab hold of his dick.

"What?" Please repeat the question I almost whisper or stop talking and fuck me instead.

"Have you ever done any modeling?" He pivots back on his heel now and I instantly feel as though the room has been deluged with an abundance of oxygen. I can breathe. I can think again.

"Why?" Answering a question with a question is something I retrieve from my bag of lame tricks whenever I feel overwhelmed by a man. It doesn't happen often, but let's face it; the Noah Foster isn't your everyday kind of man.

"You're gorgeous." His lips curl into another dazzling smile. "I've been looking for someone just like you."

My libido jumps at the announcement. Wait? He's been looking for someone just like me? As in, a woman with long blonde hair and blue eyes who apparently looks like a hooker who delivers sandwiches? "For what?" I raise a brow. If I don't ask, I'm never going to know.

"For my next project."

I lick my lips wondering if his next project involves me getting as naked as he still is. "What kind of project?"

The shrill bite of a ringing phone cuts through the space. "I have to get that." He turns to walk down the hallway towards what looks like a multitude of doorways. "Wait right there."

I use the momentary reprieve to fetch my own phone from my bag and pull open the browser. If I'm lucky I can get in a quick search of who the Noah Foster is before he comes bouncing back down the marble corridor towards me. My knees buckle, my heart pounds and my entire body flushes as I scan the results. This is a world I have absolutely no interest in. My mother taught me not to be impolite but there's no way in hell I'm sticking around to say goodbye to him.

Chapter 3

"That sandwich was for the Noah Foster?"

"The Noah Foster?" I try to stifle a laugh as I stare at Sadie's face. "You sound exactly like him."

"He's a recluse." She leans back in her chair. "No one ever sees him anymore."

The image of the scar that covers his cheek flashes back into my mind. "Anymore?"

"He just disappeared from the public…" her voice trails as she studies the pile of linen napkins she's folding. "He used to be in all the papers dating this celebrity or that one. He dated a lot of models too. Then he kind of just went underground or something. You know how those artsy types are. What did you two talk about?"

I playfully scowl at her. "Once I read that he was selling nudie pics of women for thousands of dollars I high tailed it out of there."

"You make it sound so disgusting." She pulls her head back in a laugh. "He's a very famous photographer. His pictures are in demand. They're breathtaking."

"How do you even know that?"

"Everyone knows who Noah Foster is." She tilts her head to the side so quickly, her long brown hair flits across her face. "My mom has one of his images in her library."

"That gorgeous abstract picture of a woman's back?" I ask. I've long admired the beauty in that photograph but whatever interest I had in it was fleeting. I just remember being surprised that Sadie's conservative mother would have a picture of a woman's naked back and side boob on full display.

"That's the one." She nods as her gaze travels past my head to where her husband, Hunter, is standing at the front door to their restaurant.

"Was he good to you when I was away?" I ask it teasingly although the question itself is rooted in concern. Hunter and Sadie's relationship hasn't been easy on her and now that she's married to him, I can't help but be worried about the best friend I've had since grade school. She's always been so focused on becoming a doctor, and now with a husband and stepson I worry that her own dreams will get lost within what the family needs.

"He's amazing." Her eyes catch mine. "What about you?"

I know where she's going with this and I'm not about to travel down that road with her. I'd confided in her about my brief romance while I was in Paris. The man I'd gotten involved with was bad news from the start and Sadie has warned me that I'd get burned. I wasn't in the mood for a lecture on yet another of the idiotic man choices I'd made over the years. "Noah has a scar."

She physically shudders at my statement. I want a diversion but this is a touchy subject for her and it's not fair of me to throw it at her when she's not ready. I should have warmed her up a bit.

"Like my scar." Her hand leaps to her chest and her fingers fan across it. The large scar that is the ever present reminder of her heart transplant has always caused her emotional pain. I know that. We've been almost inseparable since we were kids. Tossing Noah's scar into the middle of our conversation is something I instantly regret.

"I'm sorry," I whisper. "It's not like yours. His is on his face."

"His face?"

I nod. "He was all weird about it. He actually pointed it out to me."

"You didn't notice it?" She pushes the napkins aside and runs her hand over the tablecloth. "It can't be that noticeable then."

"I was staring at his cock so I didn't notice the scar." As soon as the words leave my mouth I realize they sound way too casual.

"What?" The question is more of a masked giggle than an actual query. The way she pulls her hand to her mouth to quiet the chuckling brings a massive smile to my face. Sadie's adorable and she's even more so when she's having fun.

I run my hands across my brow and push my hair back over my shoulders before I dive into the subject at hand. "He was naked when I got there."

"Noah Foster was naked?" The words bubble out from behind her fingers, veiling the overt giddiness in them.

I bite my bottom lip to curtail my own amusement. "He thought I was a hooker."

"A hooker?" There's no tempering her tone now. The question flies out of her with full throttle.

"Sadie." I reach across the table to grab her hand. "Don't scream it."

She leans forward before speaking. "I can't help it. You just said you saw Noah Foster naked and he thought you were a prostitute."

I nod. "One showed up while I was there."

She shakes her head from side-to-side as if she's trying to clear out a wedge of something that's lodged in her ears. "Did you just say a prostitute was there too?"

"Briefly." I whip my hand through the air as if I'm swatting away a fly, or in this case, the memory of Noah's almost companion for the night. "She left right after he paid her."

"Did you watch them having sex?"

I almost have to close my mouth manually after that question. I can literally feel my jaw drop open. "Sadie," I say as I swallow the lump in my throat. "What? Why would you ask that?"

"Alexa," she whispers in a very high tone. "You said you saw him naked and he paid a prostitute while you were there." The way her eyebrows are dancing around is unsettling. It's as though she thinks she's got a clear view of what went on in Noah's apartment. I was there and I'm still not clear on what happened.

"He didn't sleep with the hooker." I'm hoping the relief I feel when I say that isn't transparent within my tone. Why do I care who he sleeps with? I had a brief, very enticing, encounter with the seemingly famous Noah Foster. It's over now.

"So nothing happened?" she asks, disappointment edging the question.

"He said he's been looking for someone like me for his next project." It's all I've thought about since I raced home from his place and made myself come in the shower. I can't stop thinking about him. I want to be his next project. At this point in time I'm game for just about anything as long as it doesn't involve a threesome with me and one of his call girl friends. I want that man all to myself.

Sadie freezes before she opens her mouth to speak. "Noah Foster wants you to be his next project? Do you know what that means?"

I don't. I can't think about it because if I do, I'm going to ride that elevator back to his penthouse and agree to whatever he wants. "What does it mean?" I ask, already knowing full well the answer.

"He wants to photograph you, Alexa." Her tone is way too excited. "Noah Foster wants you."

Chapter 4

"This isn't funny." I push past him into the now familiar foyer of his penthouse. "Did you actually think it was funny to call the restaurant and ask for me to deliver your sandwich? I have plans."

"I tip very well." Noah reaches to pull the paper bag emblazoned with Axel Boston's logo from my grasp. "I don't like sandwiches."

I can't help but chuckle at the confession. "Why did you order one then?"

"Now or then?"

"You know you talk in riddles, right?" I turn to look at him and soak in how amazing he looks half dressed. His chiseled torso is still on full, and very welcomed, display but now he's wearing faded jeans.

"Are you asking why I ordered a sandwich tonight or two nights ago when you first showed up?" His brow pops up slightly as the words float across his lips.

"Either," I reply, unsure whether I can actually physically pull my gaze from his mouth.

"I like Bernie." It's a clear and very concise statement. That's not to say it doesn't surprise me.

"You like the delivery man?" I don't want to sound as judgmental as I do.

He stares down at his hand, picking at the nail on his index finger. "He's a good soul."

"He'll be back at work tomorrow so you two can catch up then," I offer before reaching back to grab the handle of the door. "I need to take off."

"You have plans you said?"

It's a question that catches me off guard. It's becoming increasingly apparent that in Noah Foster's world all he has to do is ask for something and it magically appears. When Sadie texted me to tell me that he wanted me to personally deliver his sandwich I froze. Her insistence that I give in and help with his next project was a waste of her breath. I can't. I won't. After researching him more, and discovering the careless way he uses women, I know that I don't belong in his world.

"I do." I'm not going to fill in the blanks. Why should I bother? He's obviously got more than one call girl on speed dial. He doesn't need me here.

"Cancel the plans." His shoulders tense as he shifts on his feet in front of me.

I step forward, challenging him. "No. I won't cancel."

"You know more about me now than when you took off the other night." A ghost of a smile flashes across his face. "I take it you researched who I am."

"The Noah Foster." I pull air quotes around the words. "Photographer extraordinaire."

His eyes dance as his name skirts across my lips. "Tell me more."

I scowl at the request. He's so full of himself that he actually wants me to recite his life story back to him. "You're twenty-nine and very elusive. You have a showing once a year and your pictures sell for a lot of money."

"Impressive, Alexa." His eyes darken. "You also researched this, no?" The careless way his hand brushes over his cheek is telling. I've seen Sadie do it a million times before when talking about her scar.

"No," I lie. I had tried in vain to find out what happened to his face, but there was nothing out there. I couldn't find a drop of information about the scar or what had caused it. "That I don't care about."

"You're lying."

"It's just a scar, the Noah Foster." I bite the edge of my tongue to temper my amusement. "You don't actually think anyone cares about it, do you?"

His expression shifts as his eyes gloss over. "You wouldn't understand."

I'm not about to tiptoe around this. "I understand. My best friend has a scar."

"She'd understand."

I ignore the inference that I'm not compassionate enough to understand what he feels. "If we're done here I need to get to a club. I'm meeting friends."

"We're not done." He steps into my path. "I wanted to see you again before I made my decision."

"Riddles, Noah." I push on his chest, shaken by the energy that instantly flows between the two of us. "What decision?"

"There's a part of me that wants to photograph you for my next showing." He holds out his left hand as if he's offering it to me. "The other part of me really wants to fuck you." His right hand darts out.

Somehow I find my voice that is now buried in wanton desire. "You're assuming I want either." I want both. Can I have both pretty please?

"You want both," he counters.

I close my eyes tightly. I'm certain that something that has flashed across my expression is speaking to him the same way a bright neon sign would. "No," I whisper back. "I don't want either."

"You've researched me. You like my work." His tone is so confident and smooth. It's both irritating and alluring. Why the hell am I still standing here listening to him? Why haven't I bolted past him and hopped in a taxi to take me to the club?

"Your work is interesting," I say in a tempered tone. "I didn't know a thing about it until yesterday."

"I like that about you." His hand skirts over the hem of my white dress. "You don't give a shit about who I am, do you?"

I tip my brow in response. "You're right," I say coolly. "I don't give a shit about who you are."

"I want you to be the focus of my new show." He cocks his head as his eyes travel over my face. "You're perfect."

"I'm not interested." The sudden realization that this may actually be happening has dampened my desire to pose nude for him. That was just a fleeting fantasy I was having when I was masturbating to thoughts of him standing above me in all his naked glory holding a camera in one hand. I need to find a way to have less convoluted dreams.

"I'll pay you." Enticement skirts the words. "A lot," he adds for extra measure.

I hesitate. I know he sees it in my expression. I study his brown eyes, admiring the length of the lashes. There's a small mole beside his left eye, just above the scar. I stare at him wondering whether he'd be as seductive without the scar. It adds an edge to him that makes him utterly irresistible.

"Thousands, Alexa," he presses. "I'll pay you thousands of dollars if you'll pose for me."

My sex aches at the thought of diving into an arrangement like that with him. He must fuck the women he photographs. He's so raw and determined. "I'm going to be a teacher," I almost whimper. I can't do something like that.

"I don't photograph faces." His eyes follow the path of his index finger as it runs across my chin. "You won't be identifiable. It will be our little secret."

"No one will know?"

"No one." His breath hitches as his finger settles on my bottom lip. "You'll sign a non-disclosure agreement as will I."

"I can't talk about it to anyone?" My voice is getting higher with excitement. If no one is going to find out, what's the harm? I can definitely use the money and the idea of spending any time alone with him is too tempting a proposition to pass on. It's also the perfect way to chase away memories of Paris and the mess I'd made of my life there. I'm totally game for this.

He flashes a smile. "No one and there's one more thing before you agree."

My stomach drops. "What?"

"I don't fuck my models." The words are clear, direct and there's no compromise woven into them at all.

My heart lurches at the announcement. "You never fuck any of the women who model for you?"

"Never."

"Ever?" I ask quietly.

He stops himself just as his mouth opens to speak. He shakes his head slightly as if to ward off one thought to replace it with another. "Once you sign that form, it's all business, no pleasure."

"Where's the dotted line?" I hear my voice asking the question, although my body is begging me to turn him down.

Chapter 5

"Do you wax?" He looks past the bed to where I'm sitting in an oversized leather chair.

It's an intimate question but given the fact that I signed my body away to him yesterday, it's useless to try and play coy at this point. "I do."

"Brazilian? French?" He tips his head towards my skirt.

"Brazilian," I blush. "I like the way it feels."

His brow cocks at my response as he runs his hand over the white sheet he just placed on the king size bed. "Are your tits real?"

My arms jump across my chest in subconscious defense. "They're real," I whisper. What the hell have I gotten myself into? I'm in the bedroom of a hot-as-hell guy who is once again almost naked and nothing is going to happen other than him taking a few pictures of my body. I'm going to need to find a man to fuck after this is over.

"Take off your clothes." He doesn't shift his gaze from the camera that's now in his hands as he barks the order in my direction.

I stand and slip my feet out of my heels. "I thought we could ease into this, Noah."

"Alexa," he pauses briefly. "I've seen it all before. Let's get moving before we lose all our natural light."

I stare absentmindedly at the windows of his condo. There's nothing shuttering the light at all. "You don't have any blinds or curtains," I say it aloud even though I meant to keep the statement to myself.

"I like the city." He glances towards the ceiling to floor windows. "I like how authentic the world is without any masks."

"I thought you were just lazy," I mutter in response, half hoping that he doesn't hear me.

"Clothes off, Alexa." He pushes his jeans to the ground and his almost erect cock once again springs into full view. I've seen this man naked more in the past few days than most men I've been involved with.

"Why are you naked?" I ask before my brain can process how senseless the question is. Why do I care whether he's naked? It's a bonus. A very welcome, perfectly shaped, and super-size bonus.

"I work better without constraints." His voice lacks any emotion at all. Obviously when he's in the zone, he's firmly planted there and that's the end of that. "You're wasting my time. Get out of your clothes now."

If he was so eager to get me in the raw because he was going to fuck my brains out I'd be all over it, but the fact that he's pushing me so he can capture my nude body on a memory card is much less appealing. Why am I doing this? Is five thousand dollars really worth this?

I pull the navy sweater I'm wearing over my head as my eyes trail a path behind him. His firm, round ass is right there. I can almost reach out and grab it. I close my eyes to chase away thoughts of my nails digging into it as he's buried in my body taking me to the very edge of pleasure. I've never had a cock that size inside of me. I've never wanted a cock as much as I want his, or him. Whatever, Alexa. You're here for a job, so just do it.

I push my gaze down to my pencil skirt as I pull the side zipper down. I step out of it just as the room fills with the low sound of classical music. Great, he's a Beethoven buff who likes to work in the buff. I don't look up as I unhook the front clasp of my bra and then quickly push my white lace panties to the floor. This is it. Your mother would be so freaking proud of you right now, Alexa. She did warn you about strangers but you never listen to her.

"Fuck me, Alexa." The low growl of his voice instantly pours into me. "Christ, you're gorgeous."

I pull in a heavy breath before I look at him. His cock has sprung to full attention and I briefly wonder if I can void our agreement and just sit on his lap right here and right now. "What now?" I sound anxious. It makes sense given the fact that my heart is beating so wildly in my chest that I can't help but wonder if the people in the apartment below him can hear the rhythmic pounding of it.

"Get on the bed." He points to the middle of the bed and I settle myself there, unsure of anything else.

"Like this?" I ask tentatively. I wish I could redo the past day. When he'd handed me the non-disclosure agreement and contract stating that I gave him free rein to take as many images as he wants, I saw it as an adventure I'd likely never get the chance to partake in again. Now, I just feel awkward and uncomfortable.

"Lay back." He moves to the side of the bed and gently guides my shoulder down. "Just relax. I'm going to take a few test shots for lighting."

I nod in agreement and push my back into the bed, before I pull my hands over my stomach. I desperately want to cover my breasts but it will do little good. My entire, nude body is on full display and he's focused intently on his camera. I hear the distinctive sound of the shutter clicking as he takes one image after another before studying the results.

"The lighting is just right." He leaps onto the bed in one swift movement. "You need to relax." He peers out from behind the camera to lock eyes with me.

That's much easier said than done. I'm sprawled out completely exposed on his bed while he towers over me with his dick bobbing madly in the air in response to every single movement he makes.

"I'm trying," I whisper through clenched teeth. If I can just stop looking at him, I'll be able to focus on the task at hand. I can't think about sex. I can't think about coming. I can't think about anything but posing for him.

"When's the last time you were fucked, Alexa?"

Well, hell. Now what?

Chapter 6

"You can't ask me that." I spring up from the bed into a sitting position. I'm suddenly even more aware of how visible every inch of me is right now.

He teeters back on his heels trying to regain his footing on the mattress. "Whoa, calm down. It's just a question."

I reach aimlessly for any part of a sheet that I can use to cover myself. I knew this was a mistake. My inner good girl was screaming at me that I'd regret this. I'm not five minutes in and I'm wishing I could dive under the bed and hide. I don't want to talk about sex with him. I want to *have* sex with him. "You didn't say anything about personal questions." I don't actually sound as freaked out over this as I feel, do I?

"I was trying to get you to relax." He drops to his knees now and I can literally almost reach out and brush my lips against his. He looks so devastatingly alluring. Why am I not having sex with him right now?

"By asking me about my sex life?"

"Alexa." His hand grazes across my shoulder. "This is a process. I need you to relax and talking about sex helps people relax."

"What people?" I push my arm across my breasts to cover them at the very same moment I pull my knees to my chest. I'm not going for attractive right now. I'm going for coverage and this stance, albeit awkward, is working for me.

"Women." His tongue flits over his lips. "When a woman talks about the men she's slept with, her body changes."

"Changes?" I swallow hard to stave off the increasing dryness that is overtaking my mouth. I'm so parched. I feel as though I'm sitting in the middle of a desert with absolutely nothing in sight to satiate me.

He studies me with a furrowed brow as he stands to reach for a chilled bottle of water sitting atop a small table by the window. "Here." He twists the cap to open it before shoving it harshly into my hand.

I greedily take it from him and swallow half the bottle in a single gulp. My teeth finally feel as though they aren't glued to the inside of my lips. "What changes?" I repeat, not wanting to miss the answer that I'm sure will make little to no sense to me. His curiosity about my last lover has nothing to do with our photo shoot. I know I'm right about that.

"I asked the wrong question." He leans back and rests one hand on the bed. "Let's start with your most memorable lover."

I crease my forehead in confusion. "No." I shake my head. "Let's start with why you think it's necessary to talk about the men I've fucked."

I fully expect him to dodge the question yet again but he surprises me. "You'll relax if you share."

"I don't think so." I have to temper a laugh. "My sexual past isn't your business."

He leans forward again so he's close enough for me to touch. "I don't give a shit about it, Alexa. The details are irrelevant to me."

The words bite. "Why ask then?"

"You'll open up more if you share." The corner of his lip twitches slightly. "It will help you feel less vulnerable and more in control of what we're doing. It's part of my process."

His process? Asking me intimate details about my past lovers is part of his process? That makes about as much sense as my being here in the first place.

"You're strange," I mutter as I lean back on the bed. "Let's just get this over with."

He's back on his feet again, his cock lazily hanging in my direction. "The lover you can't forget, Alexa. Tell me about him."

"That would be Nathan."

Chapter 7

"Tilt your head to the left." He motions towards my left with his index finger as he points the camera directly at my chest.

"Why my head?" I bolt back to a sitting position. "You said no face shots."

He stalls and pulls the camera down to reveal his face. "Your chin may be visible in some shots. You don't have a problem with that, do you?" His tone is skirting on the edge of frustration.

I don't push knowing that each time I interrupt him means more time spent naked on his bed with his camera hovering over me. I fall back onto the sheet, pulling my arms lazily over my head.

"Tell me about Nathan." His index finger once again motions to the left and I shift my face to the side.

"What about him?" I ask back. Before today, Nathan was someone I hadn't thought about in months. He was a random I picked up in a club. He was gorgeous, fantastic in bed and a fleeting moment of time in my life. I know nothing about him. I never got his last name or what he did for a living.

"Was he your boyfriend?" He stares at me through the camera lens for several seconds. I know he's gauging my reaction. I know he's chasing the perfect shot.

I try to temper my chuckle. "Nathan? He's not a boyfriend."

"What does that mean?" His voice is low and uncompromising.

"Nathan is a one night stand guy. He doesn't do relationships, just random fucks." I push my cheek into the sheet to hide the blush I feel wafting over my face. "We hooked up at a club."

"When?"

"It was a long time ago." I adjust my legs to try and hide any hint of arousal that may be rushing to the surface. "I guess about three years ago now."

"You were old enough to go to a club three years ago?" His finger slides to the right and juts into the air. "Shift your hips to the right."

I push my heels into the bed as I move my body. "I had fake ID," I confess.

"How old were you?"

"I was nineteen then," I groan. I'd felt so mature back then.

He pulls the camera down to look directly at me. "So you fucked him that one time?"

I nod as I feel the rush of arousal spread to my breasts. My nipples harden under his gaze. "He fucked me five or six times that night." I'd lost track after the first. It was the only time in my life I'd come more than once in a row.

"You compare every other man to him, don't you?" It's not meant to sound challenging, but it does. At the very least, that's how I absorb it.

"I did at first," I say as honestly as I can. "I actually kept going back to that club to try and find him again to fuck."

"Did you?"

"Did I fuck him again?" My hand twitches at the thought of Nathan's skilled body inside of mine. I want to touch myself right now thinking about it.

"Did you find him again?" His eyes fall to my legs and I know that he's wondering if I'm as aroused as I sound.

"No." The defeat in my voice is evident. "I heard he moved to New York so that was the end of that."

"You think about him when you get yourself off, don't you?" he growls. "You close your eyes when other men are fucking you and you think about his dick being inside of you."

I almost moan at the sound of the words. "Yes," I whimper under my breath as I slide my legs apart. "Yes." I've fucked dozens of men since then in pursuit of the high I felt that night.

"Like that, Alexa." His voice fades into the distance as I close my eyes and run my tongue over my lips thinking about the one night stand I'll never forget.

Chapter 8

"When are you going to schedule your practicum, Lexi?" she asks, knowing full well that I haven't liked the nickname since I was seven-years-old.

"Why do you insist on calling me that?" I bark back. I'm tired of it. I thought that after I returned from Paris, my mother would have a newfound respect for me. She was the one who told me I'd never survive a month there, and I'd lasted more than half a year.

She shakes her head as if to ward off my question. "The practicum? When are you scheduling that?"

It was an important step towards my degree in education and before I'd stumbled into Noah Foster's life it had been on the top of my priority list. Now, I was so caught up in the idea of posing nude for him, that I'd pushed my actual career to the side. That needed to change today. "I'll arrange that today." It's a definitive answer that I plan to back up with action. In fact, if I leave now I can not only avoid a dessert course with my overbearing mother, but the midday traffic that clogs up the arteries around Boston too.

"What are you doing for money?" She taps her hand on the table in the upscale restaurant she dragged me to for lunch. "I thought you'd go back to working at the bistro when you got back."

My part-time job at Star Bistro being a barista had been fun when Sadie worked there with me. Now that she was married to the man whose family owned many restaurants along the east coast, serving coffee wasn't on her radar. I assumed I'd fall back into that routine after Paris, but my modeling job with Noah had changed all that. He was paying me enough that I didn't have to work, at least for the immediate future. I knew I'd need to start considering my options in the next few weeks though.

"I might look for something in child care," I say it as much to stun my mother as to appease my need to be around children. At first glance, I'm not exactly the type of woman that you'd immediately peg as being a kid person, but I love them and since I'm not qualified to teach just yet, helping out at a daycare or after school program seems ideal.

"Seriously?" She doesn't even try and disguise her surprise.

"Seriously," I repeat back as I stand and reach over to kiss her cheek. "I've got to run, mom. I'll talk to you next week."

With that, my parent quota for the week is officially filled without her having even the slightest inkling about what I and my naked body have been up to.

***

"You're going to tie me to that bed?" I point at the bed as if I'm trying to distinguish between it and an invisible bed within the bedroom room we're standing in. This bedroom, which is down the hall from the one we were in last time, is darker, edgier and actually has window coverings. "Noah, you never said anything about bondage."

"Your contract includes bondage." He glances back at me briefly as he sets up a light next to the four poster bed. "It's scarves, Alexa. They're for show."

"For show?" I peel my jeans off before slipping out of my black panties. This is only the second time he's seen me naked but I've already learned the valuable lesson that wasting Noah Foster's precious time only makes him cranky. If I cooperate fully, I'll be out of the bindings and this room early enough that I can meet my friend Kayla at a bar downtown.

He nods without turning his attention to me. I should take offense at the fact that he doesn't flinch at the sight of my naked body, but I've gotten over that. It's all about getting down to business now and getting this gig over and done with so I can move on with my life, money in hand.

"Get on the bed." He sounds more callous than last time, if that's even possible.

"In the middle?" I push myself to the center of the bed before resting my back against the very uncomfortable mattress.

He shakes his head impatiently. "How can the bindings reach if you're way down there?" He grabs my upper arm and yanks hard on it.

I wince as I pull it free. "Fuck, Noah. That hurt."

"I'm sorry." The words are barely audible and instantly leave me wondering if they are foreign to him. He doesn't strike me as the type of man that offers amends often. "You need to move up." He pats the mattress next to me. "Move your ass up here."

I scoot my naked body up towards the heavy, wooden headboard, painfully aware that his eyes are fixed on my bouncing tits. "Here?" I tilt my head down as I ask the question, wanting to catch his gaze.

He doesn't take the hint and for the first time, I feel vulnerable under his watchful eyes.

"Noah?" I whisper his name not wanting to call too much attention to the fact that he's frozen in place. "Is this good?"

His eyes travel slowly up my body before they land squarely on my face. "You're beautiful, Alexa."

I try not to smile too broadly at the compliment even though it means more coming from him than I'd ever admit. Regardless of the fact that we have a written agreement that clearly states that we aren't going to engage in anything beyond picture taking, knowing that he finds me beautiful, stirs up something deep within me.

"You're not bad yourself," I offer back. I should tell him that he's the hottest man I've ever been naked with but that would be pushing my luck and pushing buttons that aren't going to get me what I want. He's never going to fuck me into tomorrow. It's just not going to happen.

"It really doesn't bother you, does it?" He settles onto the bed next to me, his strong, tattooed chest just inches from my touch.

"What?" I can't form a coherent response. Even though he's wearing jeans, he's still exuding more raw lust than any man I've ever met. I know that if he fucked me, Nathan would become a distant memory of my second best lay and my time in Paris would cease to exist in my mind.

"The scar." His voice cracks as the word leaves his lips. "My scar."

Chapter 9

"You can't tie me to the bed and then ask me something like that." I protest too weakly. He hears it within my voice just as much as I do. The only grace that he's offered me tonight is the fact that he hasn't yet tied my ankles to the bed. I'm not sure if it was intentional or if he did it to watch me squirm after asking me a question like that.

"It's a simple question, Alexa. Do you like sucking cock?"

"I'm pretty sure you can get a woman to open up to you…" my voice trails as he slips out of his jeans. "Or whatever your process is without asking her whether she likes blowing guys. Besides, I asked about your scar and you completely ignored that."

His full lips turn into a sly grin as he picks up his camera and sits next to me. "Do you?"

"Riddles," I pull the word slowly across my tongue before I lick my bottom lip. "You speak in riddles, Noah."

His finger jumps to my chin and I groan without thinking as it traces a path across my jaw. "Tilt your head this way, Alexa," he says softly. "I want to capture your bottom lip. It's perfect."

I try and push my face into the opposite side of the bed, but he holds steadily to my chin. "You said you wouldn't take pictures of my face," I whimper. "My lips. People might know."

"The only people who would know, Alexa…" His warm, heavy breath grazes over my chest before he continues, "Are the men you've sucked off. No one could forget these lips."

I close my eyes trying to ward off the thought of his cock sliding between my lips. I've wanted that since he flung open the door to his apartment the first night we met. I can't exactly tell him that I've replayed that moment in my mind over and over again and almost each time I imagine dropping to my knees and sucking his cock until he shoots his load all over me.

"Alexa, your head." His finger brushes against my cheek. "Turn towards me."

I pull my eyes open slowly as I tilt my head in his direction. He's kneeling next to me now, his almost erect cock just inches from my lips. If this is a test, I'm about to fail miserably. I lick my bottom lip slowly aching to taste the large head of his dick. If I just shift my body ever so slightly, I know I can reach. Would he stop me? Would he let me?

"That's perfect," he growls as I hear the distinctive sound of the camera capturing dozens of images in a row. "Your lips are so perfect."

That's the photographer in him talking and I can't forget that as much as I want to. This has turned into a battle of me against my own will as much as a job. He's toying with me. It's what he's done from the beginning but calling him on it will only feed his already colossal ego. I read enough stories on the Internet about how he discarded countless women after being involved with them for a short time. That had to have been pre scar though. From what I've seen and witnessed, this version of Noah Foster doesn't go out much at all.

"Alexa," he calls out and I realize that I've heard him repeat my name several times now. I was drifting.

"What?" I bite back as my eyes fly open to the sight of him hovering above me, his camera in one hand. Christ, please make him stop being so utterly gorgeous. Is this some sick, twisted game of karma? You throw me into a room with a naked man who looks like this and then I can't touch him. This has to be worth more than five thousand dollars. It's like one of those credit card commercials. This is fucking priceless.

"Talk to me about your last lover." He inches down the bed so I can't make eye contact with him. Smart move, Noah. He asked this once before and my reaction then should have been enough to get him to back the hell off. There's no mistaking what a pushy son of a bitch he is.

"Let's talk about you instead," I counter, trying to veil the wide grin that has taken over my face. "What about your last lover?"

"This isn't about me." His response is curt and harsh. "I get to ask the questions."

"I don't have to answer them," I push back, pulling my legs closer together. I've had enough of this for one night and maybe shooting personal questions in his direction is going to be the ticket I need to get out of these bindings, this bed and this room for the night.

"One question, Alexa," he says with a growl. "You ask one question. I'll answer and then you let me work."

One question? Just one? I study his face and soak in the sight of his eyes staring a path straight through me. We're both naked, nothing separating us but a piece of paper that clearly states that he's never going to ravage my body the way I want him to. If I can't have that, I can definitely have something almost as good. "Tell me about your most memorable lover."

"I haven't met her yet," he begins before his voice stalls. "Or I haven't fucked her yet."

"That's a cop out." I adjust my hips to allow my legs to slide open slightly.

His eyes follow my movement and I know he's staring at my wetness. I've never minded being naked in front of a man, and with Noah, it's quickly becoming second nature. I'm not even sure what it would feel like to actually have a conversation with him while I'm fully clothed.

"You're wet." His voice is thick and heavy. "You get so wet when I'm photographing you."

I push my legs even further apart. "You're gorgeous," I admit. "I've never seen a man's body like yours."

"You get wet from looking at me?" His hand shifts from his lap to the edge of my thigh.

I have to stall my breathing to suppress a deep, guttural moan that is building within me. "You're not surprised by that." He can't be. He knows exactly what he looks like.

"I pay women to fuck me," he whispers. "They'll tell me anything to make a dollar."

"Do they tell you that you're hot as fuck?" I pull against the bindings, my hands instinctively wanting to trace a path across my folds. I'm so aroused. I want so badly to come.

"Hot as fuck?" The words rumble through him and across his lips. "No one has ever told me that."

"You're lying," I challenge. "Women tell you all the time that they want you."

"Do you want me?" It's a question that is engorged with unending consequence.

I pull my tongue across my lips, let my legs fall open to reveal how dripping wet I actually am and utter a very clear and unmistakable. "Yes."

Chapter 10

"You know I can't touch you." His breath skirts heavy over my cheek. His mouth is hovering so close to mine, his tongue darting out to moisten his lips.

"I don't follow rules." I push the words back at him. "We have a non-disclosure agreement. I wouldn't tell a soul if you touched me." The words are meant to tease him but I realize once they float over my lips that they're true. I don't follow rules. I never have. I've always chased after every man I've wanted. I've never been the quiet, demure and well behaved girl who waits to be swept off her feet. If I see something I want, I take it. Consequences come later.

"You're not my type, Alexa." I can sense he's smiling even though I can't see his face. He's too close to me. The warmth of his skin is radiating into mine.

I swallow hard as much to gather the words from within me as to calm my racing heart. "That's why you want me so much." I'm playing with fire. He's unlike any man I've ever met. He's dark, he's edgy. He obviously has more issues than I can count on one hand and he's here, so close, so hard and so wanting.

"If I touch you, it's going to ruin the process," he says it with strength of purpose. He shifts his body slightly and I feel the tip of his dick brush against my leg.

I catch my bottom lip between my teeth when I feel the ache in my sex. I'm so aroused that I'm about to come without any stimulation at all. "If you untie my hands, Noah…" I tilt my head to the side and my lips brush over his as the words leave me. "If you untie me, I'll make myself come right now."

His breathing stalls. "Alexa, you're killing me."

I close my eyes and push a rush of breath from my lungs so it seeps out of my lips and flashes over his. I want to say something but I know that anything that escapes from me at this point is going to be enveloped with a moan.

"Your skin is beautiful." His hand is back on my hip now but its intent isn't the same as it was before. His touch is softer, gentle.

There's no direction there. This time it's not to guide me into the perfect pose. This time there's something else beneath it.

I push my head closer to his and there's no hesitation in the air between us. His lips glide quickly and harshly over mine. They're soft. His kiss is so lush, so greedy and complete. I struggle beneath the bindings as he claims my mouth with his without any apology at all. The groan that travels through his body and into mine causes me to buck my hips.

"Alexa. Christ," he growls as his hand glides across my stomach towards my wetness.

I moan loudly the moment his fingers rake over my moist folds. His touch is soft at first but quickly there's a distinctive shift to something else. I grind my heels into the mattress to gain more depth of pleasure. I push my hips into his hand and I'm rewarded when he lets out a deep, guttural and purely sensual grunt.

"Fuck it." The words escape him in a rush and I feel instantly bereft when his body pulls quickly from mine.

"Noah," I whimper as I close my eyes. "Please don't stop."

"I fucking can't stop."

I scream loudly the instant I feel his tongue on me. I buck my hips up and into him. I tense when I realize I can't reach down to guide his mouth. I want to. I need to. "Untie me," I beg. "Noah, untie me."

He ignores my pleadings as his hands reach beneath me to cup my ass in his palms. His head is moving quickly, mirroring the actions of his tongue. He's eating me with a fury and passion that I've never experienced before. I'm close to coming. I can feel the depth of it building deep within me. I brace myself as he pushes my legs wider apart.

"Fuck, your pussy is so good." The words fill the heated silence in the room. They're raw and electric and push me even closer to an edge I want to fly over.

"Like that, Noah," I whisper through clenched teeth. "Just like that."

"Like this." His teeth etch a line over my clit and I race into an earth shattering climax. I buck underneath him, my body dictating my reaction. I feel the instant flow of wetness from me. He laps it up, the entire time his moans echoing through my already sensitive flesh.

Chapter 11

"I want you to…" my voice trails as he whips his tongue around the swollen bud again. "Noah, just do it."

"No." He breathes into my folds. "I'm not untying you. I'm going to fuck you just like this, Alexa."

"Untie me," I plead again. The fact that he's already made me come twice with his mouth while keeping me tied up is torture enough. I need to touch him when he slides his dick inside of me.

He pulls his massive frame across my body so he's hovering right above me, his hands pressing into the mattress on either side of my head. "It's not happening. I want you spread out just like this for me. I'm going to fuck you so hard, Alexa. So hard. My dick is going to fill you right up."

I skip a breath at the promise of it. "Let me suck your cock first," I'm begging. Can he hear that in my tone? Does he know how much I want to take him in my mouth? Can he feel that desire seeping out of every part of my body?

"If I slide my cock in that perfect mouth, I'll come right down your throat," he says gruffly. "I'm going into my bedroom to get a condom and when I get back, I'm going to fuck your beautiful tight pussy until you come all over me."

Holy fucking hell.

I clench my thighs together as I watch him round the corner and head down the hallway. I've never been taken before while bound to a bed or anything else for that matter. I'm already so close to another orgasm. I have to calm down. I have to temper my want or I'm going to scream out the second he pushes his dick into my body.

"Goddammit, you look so fucking amazing right now." He's back with a foil package in his palm.

"Put it on," I beg in a high voice. I don't care if I sound like I'm in heat right now. I want this so much. I need this more than I've needed anything in a very long time.

"Wait." He stalls and the condom package drifts lazily from his palm and onto the bed. "You're so beautiful. I need to capture this."

I can't compute what's happening. My libido is having a fight to the death with my mind. Is he actually reaching for his camera? He's going to take pictures of me right now? Um, what about the part where he fucks me senseless?

"Turn to the left." He inches against my thigh with his hand. "Alexa, to the left."

I stay frozen where I am. The defeat that is racing through my body is going to steal away any fetching image that he may think is nestled there. Before another second passes I'm reasonably sure that I'm going to look pissed, disappointed and I may even explode from pent up sexual frustration.

"Alexa?" He's pushing harder on my thigh now and the intimacy of the touch isn't helping in the least. "Roll a little to the left."

I shake my head slightly. "Are we going to fuck?" Why bother with formalities like being demure when you're tied to a hot guy's bed with a condom right next to you? All the pieces of the puzzle where I get to come again are there, I just need Noah to focus enough to put it altogether and in me now.

He darts to his feet above me and my question is instantly answered. "Your skin is gorgeous right now. It's perfect. To the left, Alexa."

I roll slightly to the left, which only ensures that the unopened condom package is now the center of my focus. "Like this?" I ask facetiously.

"Just like that," he says, completely and blissfully unaware of how disappointed I am.

Chapter 12

"You're taking off?" A bottle of beer dangles from his hand as he saunters back into what I've now coined as the room of broken dreams. Orgasmic dreams, that is.

Considering how focused he was when he was taking my picture, there's no use bringing up the almost fucking session that never happened. That large, veiny, thick ship has sailed right past my vagina. "I'm meeting a friend." Why bother offering more? He obviously got me all worked into a horny frenzy so he could take my picture. Asshole.

"A boyfriend?" He cocks a brow as he settles on the edge of the bed.

Did he seriously just ask me if I have a boyfriend? That might have been a more appropriate question before his face was buried tongue deep between my thighs. "Boyfriend?" I repeat back.

"Do you have a boyfriend?" He brings the bottle to his mouth and I watch him take a large gulp of the beer.

"No boyfriend." I chuckle half-heartedly.

"You're pissed that I didn't fuck you, aren't you?" The amusement lacing the question grates on my nerves.

He's an egomaniac. He wants to hear me tell him that my body is empty now that it will never have the pleasure of officially meeting the Noah Foster's cock. "Not at all." That actually sounded semi-sincere. I just need to keep up this veil of obscurity until I'm at the club with some random guy's hand up my skirt.

"You're lying."

Sweet Jesus, seriously? Are you actually allowed to be this in awe of yourself because you've sold a few dozen photographs worth hundreds of thousands of dollars?

"I'm not lying," I answer. To be precise, I'm not actually lying about being pissed that we didn't have sex. I am lying about the fact that I'm lying. I'm enraged that he had me wanting him so much and he could just drop it all in favor of a picture. I'm also humiliated by it.

"Where are you and your non-boyfriend going?" he asks, doing very little to hide the obvious enjoyment in his voice.

I'll use one of his signature moves and ignore the line of questioning. "How many more sessions do you think we'll need to have?"

"Why?" He's delving into my playbook now with the question in answer to a question. He's more blonde than he looks considering he's a gorgeous brunette.

"I need to focus on some school stuff." I scan my phone and look for any messages from my friend, Kayla. We're supposed to meet in less than twenty minutes downtown and I want to make sure that she's not bailing on me at the last minute too.

"What kind of school stuff?" He edges forward as if he's trying to get a glimpse of my smartphone screen.

"Just stuff." I toss my phone back into my bag. "If you could give me a rough schedule of the days and times you need me that would be great."

"I guess I could do that." He scratches his head right behind his ear before pulling his hand across his forehead. "I'll text it to you. Tomorrow, okay?"

"That's perfect."

"You're actually going to leave? You don't want to finish what we started?" His hand lazily runs over the tip of his semi-erect penis. How is it that I've never seen him with a limp dick?

I pull my gaze back to his face and think for a moment before I speak. "If it was meant to happen, it would have."

"So that's it?" There actual surprise in his voice. I'm not sure if he's trying to temper that or not, but it's obvious that he wasn't expecting me to pack up and walk out.

"That's it." I turn to leave.

"Alexa." I sense movement behind me before I feel his hand grip tightly to my elbow. "I want to fuck you."

My body reacts to the words, even if I don't want it to. This is too reminiscent of Paris. The push and pull is in my past. I need to keep it there even if it means passing on amazing sex with Noah. "I have plans, Noah." I pull my arm free. "I'm meeting an old friend. I don't have time to stick around."

He doesn't respond. It's not that I expect him to. Something deep within me has always known that *no* isn't a word he hears often.

***

"Wait, wait, wait." Kayla, one of my sorority sisters, teeters on the edge of a bar stool, with some ridiculously expensive drink perched in her hand. "You're telling me you were tied to a guy's bed and he was about to fuck you, but then changed his mind?"

Why does it sound so much worse coming from her? I guess if I had broken my non-disclosure agreement and confessed that the man in question decided to take my picture instead of fucking me that it would sound a little less pitiful. Would it? It sounds super humiliating regardless of how I spin the details.

"That's it in a nut shell." I tip my glass to her before taking a large gulp. Despite my desire to wash away the bitter taste of rejection with a strong drink, I've opted for a soda water. I'm done with ignoring what is really important in my life. Tomorrow morning, bright and early, I'm going to hit the pavement and the bus stop so I can find a job that doesn't involve taking my clothes off for tattooed jerks.

"You haven't talked much about Paris. I'm here if you need a shoulder."

"Thanks." I smile back at her. After my completely disappointing evening with Noah earlier, I needed this more than I realized. Letting go and having some fun is the perfect prescription for what ails me.

"What happened?" She asks as she leans forward to take a sip from the glass. "I thought you'd stay there and marry him."

"You didn't really think that," I tease. "You knew I couldn't stay away from you forever."

"Ah, Lex." She swats her hand across my knee. "You're a princess."

A princess? Sure. I'm a fucking princess who has now made two dumb ass, consecutive choices in men. "What about you?" A change of subject won't hurt anyone, other than me when Kayla starts rambling off about all the fun she's had while I've been gone.

"No." Her hand darts up so quickly she almost taps me across the nose. "Don't try that."

"Try what?" I lean back, determined to get out of her line of fire.

"You were broken up on the phone when you called me from there." She taps her hand on my knee. "I'm here to talk. Spill it."

I want to. I haven't talked to anyone, including Sadie, about what happened in Paris. Given the fact that Sadie's husband was engaged to someone else when they met, it wasn't fair to dredge all that up by throwing my relationship woes in her direction. At least, in her case, Hunter didn't love the woman he almost married before her. In my case, it's an entirely different story.

"He was involved with another woman." I've practiced saying those words so many times that now that I've actually uttered them aloud, they sound distant, misplaced and much less intense than they feel.

"What?" Kayla's shriek pulls me back to the reality of the statement. I'd confided to her in texts and phone calls that I was in love with the man in Paris. She knows that. Trying to temper it now isn't going to help me get over it. "How did you find out?"

"I saw them." I bite my lip to quash the memory of that morning. I'd just crawled out of my bed and was searching for him when I ran down to the corner café to fetch a latte. That's when I saw them together. His arm lovingly wrapped around her waist, her hand cradling his chin as she kissed him.

"Did you confront them?" She leans forward as if that's going to pull all the sordid details from deep within me.

I shake my head slightly. "No." I want to expand. I want to tell her that I couldn't do it. I want to tell her why but I can't. I won't. He set me up. He knew I went to that café every single morning. He knew that I'd show up there and that's why he brought her there, so I'd see them together and so he could see the look of utter disillusionment on my face. It took me weeks to realize that he did it because it fed something inside of him.

"So you haven't talked to Beck since?"

I sit up straighter, consciously aware of how his nickname impacts me. "We've talked but it's over."

"I'm sorry, Lex." She jumps off the stool to pull me into a warm embrace. "I'm really sorry."

Chapter 13

"You may just have the best looking ass on the planet."

Yeah, yeah, sure. I roll my eyes as I tuck my face further into the soft sheet on Noah's bed. "You say that to all the girls," I mutter under my breath.

"Did you say something?" he asks just as I feel the bed shift next to me. "What was that?"

"Are we just doing ass shots today?" I toss back. I need to keep this arrangement strictly on a business level. There's no way in hell that I'm going to allow myself to get back into a position where Noah's cock is anywhere near entering my body in any capacity. That should cover all bases.

"You said you were dealing with some school stuff."

I nod. I don't want to share any details of my life with him. He doesn't care and as soon as I do share, I'm going to be disappointed. This is a job. It's just like when I worked at Star Bistro, minus the hot guy and his impressive oral skills.

"Is that all you've got going on?" he asks as I hear the click of the camera. I know he's fishing for information about whether I hooked up with another guy since I left his place the other night. The answer to that question is a resounding and unequivocal no.

"Why aren't you asking if I like anal?" In any other circumstance that would be a conversation ender, not starter, but I am on my stomach, completely nude in the bed of one of the only men on the planet who can talk so openly about sex without being sued for harassment.

Any movement beyond my own stops and his breathing stalls. "Did you just say something about anal?"

"You were about to. I just beat you to it." I toss my head to the side so I can glance up at him. I work to level my gaze at his face instead of his ever growing penis. Would it really be that hard to take a decent picture with a pair of boxer briefs on?

"I assure you, I wasn't." He cocks a brow and lazily runs his hand over the length of his dick.

Fuck me. I can't be looking at that. I twist my head back to a forward position, instantly regretful that I looked in his direction at all.

"That's not part of your process?" I pull air quotes around the words, which isn't easy considering I'm certain I look like a beached whale at this point.

"My process varies from day-to-day." The words accompany a major shift on the mattress and I realize he's now down on his knees.

I try to move my body slightly to the right to gain distance from his leg, which is now pressing against mine. The hand on my hip stops that in its tracks.

"How long have you been doing this?" I ask after pulling my arms under my head. I wish I had thought ahead enough to grab a pillow. This position is becoming uncomfortable fast.

"Taking pictures?" It's a rhetorical question but it sucks up a few seconds of time. I'm grateful for that. I've been fishing blindly for the last hour for any subject to talk about that doesn't involve what didn't happen between us the other night. According to the text message he sent me two days ago, after today I only have to be subjected to his company two more times. I can see the finish line and my five thousand dollars in the very near distance.

"Yes. When did you get interested in it?" The words float from my lips without any curiosity attached to them. I already know the answer. After meeting Kayla at the bar, I had spent hours that night researching more about him. I'd watched a video on a website that was filmed years ago in which he spoke eloquently about his love of photography. It was difficult to watch. He was scar free, much younger and had a very carefree air about him. The barrier that was an integral part of his demeanor now didn't seem to exist back then.

"When I was a kid..." his voice trails into the distance, as I close my eyes, drifting into a place of utter silence and solitude.

Chapter 14

The now too familiar sound of a picture being taken rouses me from a dream. My eyes flutter open and I'm instantly assaulted with the lens of a camera, mere inches from my face. I push at it without thinking.

"Hey. Don't." His voice is soft and calm. There's a playful edge to it that is unfamiliar to me.

"Noah?" I push the camera aside now and he's there, right there. He's kneeling next to the side of the bed. "You can't take pictures of my face."

"These are only for me." He pushes a button on the camera and stares at it. I know he's checking the images he just took. I recognize the focused intent on his face.

"I fell asleep." I clear my throat to chase away the rumbling purr that's there. "I'm sorry."

He places the camera down next to me before resting his chin on the side of the bed. "Your body is so perfect. I got all the shots I need."

A wave of disappointment rushes through me even though those were the words I've longed to hear. It meant that I didn't need to come here anymore. It meant we had no reason to see one another. "So we're done?"

"No." His index finger pushes a stray hair back from my forehead. "We're not done. We're done for today."

I don't say anything. I'm not sure why I reacted so strongly to the idea of being done with him. I'm days away from that now. I want this to be done, don't I?

"Are you going to the show when it opens?" He taps his index finger on my arm. "I think you should be there."

"Will you be there?" I counter back. I haven't even entertained the idea of going to his show. Seeing my own naked body on full display isn't on my bucket list.

He pulls his full lips into a straight line. "I haven't decided yet."

"You don't go out at all, do you?" The fact that his coffee table is always littered with take-out boxes, and the call girl who arrived almost at the same time as me that first night, were both glaring signs of his preference for being at home. Everything he needed to be satiated was delivered right to his doorstep.

He rests his chin on the bed as his eyes scan my face. "Would you go out if your face looked like mine?"

"You know that it looks different to you than anyone else." I don't meet his eye. I can't. I don't want him to see any of the lingering desire that I still feel for him. I can't temper that. I've tried to since I came into his apartment, but it's futile.

"How so?" His brow softens.

"When I look at you it's just part of your face." I pull my hand into a tight fist to ward off the temptation to reach out and graze my fingers along the scar. "It doesn't take anything away from how you look, it adds to it."

He stills as if he's absorbing the words. I expect a dismissive retort. I assume he's going to tell me that I can't measure how it feels. He doesn't flinch as his eyes dart from my face to my lips and back again. "Tell me about your friend. You said she has a scar."

"On her chest," I offer. "She had a heart transplant."

"That's easier to accept."

I know the intention of his words. "Because she can hide it under her clothing?"

"That and…" he begins before he stalls to take a heavy swallow. "The circumstances."

"The circumstances?" I push myself up so my head is resting against my hand.

"I fell in love with a woman once," he whispers the words softly. "She loved someone else."

I sigh heavily. He's going to confess something to me now. He's going to pull down the wall that surrounds him and let me beyond it. If that happens, the entire dynamic of this is going to shift to a place where I'll want him as desperately as I did the other night when he had me bound to his bed.

"He found out about me and this happened." His hand touches his cheek over the scar. "And this…" His other hand rests just above the large tattoo that adorns his shoulder. "And this…" His hand slides to his chest and yet another intricate tattoo that I've become familiar with when I've stared at him.

I lean closer to him on the bed, not caring that my breasts have popped out from beneath the sheet that he draped over me. "You were stabbed?" My voice is barely audible as I study his body, noticing the thin raised scars that transverse his shoulder, his arm and his chest.

He only nods in response. "It was easy to cover these." His chin tilts down. "Not so easy to cover this." The hand that is still resting on his cheek quivers slightly.

"You hide because of that?" I want desperately to reach out to cover his hand with my own but I can't do that. I won't allow myself to get that close to him. I know that he can't be vulnerable. I know that he doesn't want to be.

"It's not hiding." There's no anger in his tone, only quiet clarification. "It's a reminder of something I'll never have again."

"What?"

He pulls his lips into a thin line. "I chase perfection. It's why I'm the way I am."

Before this conversation I'd absorb that statement as swollen arrogance but not now. "You want perfection because you don't think you'll ever be perfect?"

"I used to be." He sounds distant. "I'm not now."

"No one is." It's not only the right thing to say, it's the truth. In his convoluted, world famous photographer mind he may think he was once perfect, but that's simply not true. Hasn't anyone ever told him that before?

"I once was." He stalls as his eyes scan my face. "I once was as perfect as you."

Chapter 15

"I'm far from perfect." I smile broadly. "Very, very far."

"I chose you for my show because you're perfect. Everything about you speaks to me in that way." It's meant to be a compliment. At any other moment, I'd completely absorb it that way. I want to absorb it that way. I want it to bear the meaning that it's meant to but it doesn't. The words are clouded by the fact that he made a conscious decision not to make love to me when I was tied to his bed. My body was literally dripping with wanton and tangible desire for him.

"If I was perfect you would have fucked me," I say clearly. The words sound brash and violent coming from my lips. There's an undeniable attack within them. It's not directed towards him as much as myself. The rejection that I felt that night mirrored what I'd been feeling for weeks after my lover in Paris chose to unhinge me emotionally by tricking me into seeing him with the woman who owned his heart. His public display of affection destroyed all of my self-esteem and being denied Noah's body has only multiplied the emotional impact of that tenfold.

"I couldn't fuck you." He reaches across the bed to cover my hand with his. "I couldn't let myself do it."

"Why?" My voice is cracking because everything inside of me is suddenly off balance. I had vowed not to bring this up with him. I had promised myself that I wouldn't dwell on it and instead would show up, pose and get the hell out of his life.

"One taste of you unravelled me completely. If I would have fucked you that night that would have been the end of me."

"You're too dramatic," I say half-teasingly. I want the room to have more air. I need to have more space to think and feel. "You didn't fuck me because you wanted to take my picture."

"No." He slides his body from the floor into the bed next to me. "I didn't fuck you because I'd never let you go if I did."

"You're a horrible liar." I push myself to the very edge of the bed to try and gain distance from him and his sudden pronouncements of unending desire for me. What the hell happened when I fell asleep?

"I want you so badly, Alexa." His tongue darts across his lips as the words flow from them. "I really want you."

"You want me?" I push my ass even closer to the edge. I'm about ready to tumble out and onto the hardwood floor. "You don't actually want me, Noah."

"I do." He edges closer. I can feel the warmth of his body radiating against mine.

I'm inches away from falling into him and his lips. I have to pull myself together and get out of here before he decides he needs one more money shot for his gallery show next week.

"I can't do this." I press my hand against his rock hard chest. "We can't."

His arm leaps beneath the sheet to circle my waist. "Give me a reason why."

"You're playing me." I want the words to sound simple and straightforward. I want him to know that I realize that along with great picture taking skills, he's a master of manipulation.

"No." His hand traces a path across my bare hip. "I'm not playing."

"You don't fuck your models." I repeat back word-for-word what he said to me right before I signed the contract stipulating that he could take as many nude photos of me as he pleased.

"You said you break rules." The question floats across his lips with a raised brow. "Tell me that you don't want to know what it's like to feel my cock inside of your body, Alexa. Say it."

I lick my lips as the mention of his dick. He knows that I want it. My body has betrayed me endlessly since we began this wickedly tempting dance that he calls a photography project. "You know I can't say that."

"Tell me what you want." His eyes are focused completely on my mouth. "Say it, Alexa."

"No." I shake my head slightly. He wants me to confess that I want him right now. He wants me to utter the words and then he's going to grab his camera, take a round of photos and send me on my way.

"Did you fuck another guy the other night when you left here?" he asks, his eyes boring into mine. "Did you leave here and take another guy into your bed because I didn't fuck you?"

"That's none of your business," I spit back.

"I can't stop thinking about fucking you, Alexa." He shifts his body effortlessly so he's almost above me now. "I really want to fuck you."

"You're going to get me all worked up." I push my hands into his arms. "When you do you'll take another picture of me."

"I won't touch my camera until you come."

Now there's a promise that I wish I could bet on. I stare at his face, soaking in the chiseled features. His nose is slender, straight and strong. His jawline is uncompromising and full. The scar that weaves a path down his cheek is unmistakable, even though he hasn't shaved in days. He's beautiful, marred and completely unreadable.

"Let me have you." His voice is deep, dark and filled with a need that I feel within my own body. "Let me fuck you, Alexa. Now."

My mind screams at me to stop, my heart tells me that this can't end well but my body...my body slides over his as I give in to what we both need, want and have to have.

Chapter 16

"Don't move your hands, Alexa." His voice trails over my breast right before his teeth sink into the flesh over my nipple. "I'm going to fuck you just like this."

I grip harder to the pillow above my head. I scream at the assault of tender pain that comes beneath his mouth. "Don't bite me, Noah," I whisper. "No."

He ignores my trembling plea and pulls my engorged nipple between his perfect teeth. The razor sharp taste of exquisite pain races through my body at warp speed crashing directly into my core. My legs fall open involuntarily just from the sheer weight of my desire.

"I'm going to make you so wet." His hand runs up my thigh and traces a path over my folds. "I've never been with a woman who got so wet. It's fucking amazing."

I moan at the sensation of his skilled hands on my flesh. He's going to make me forget everything I want and need to forget. Christ, if his mouth and hands are any indication of his skill as a lover I'm going to forget my own name. "Please fuck me." I can't temper any of this. My body is physically aching for contact with his.

I feel him shift on the bed and I look down to the condom package in his hand. This is the point where we stalled last time. If we can just get over this hurdle, I'm finally going to get the brass ring or in this case, the perfect, large cock inside of me.

"Your pussy is so wet. Look at how it drips." He finishes rolling the condom over him before he dips his hand back between my legs. I watch with baited breath as he runs the moisture over his dick.

"Oh, God," I whisper. "Now, Noah."

"Now." He pulls my legs apart and sits between them, his full cock resting in his hand. "I've never fucked a woman like you before. Christ, how am I not going to blow my load as soon as I get inside of that?"

I twist my hips as if to beckon him closer but he's already there. I feel the full tip on me. I arch my back off the bed to try and pull it in. I need it. I don't care what happens between us after this moment in time. I just want him.

"Goddamn." He spits out through clenched teeth as he slides his cock into me.

I shudder at the girth. It's already so much, so full and so good.

His arm wraps around my right leg as he hoists it up allowing more room within my channel. A deep grunt comes pouring out of his body as he plunges balls deep into me.

I come instantly from the assault. My muscles clench tightly around his cock. I claw at his arms, wanting him to still briefly so I can soak in all the pleasure.

"Christ, Alexa." His lips course hot over mine. "You fucking came already, didn't you?"

I can only nod into the kiss as I pull his lip between my teeth.

"You're the hottest thing ever." He pulses his hips into me, his cock touching a spot deep within me. Each thrust is an exquisite mixture of pain and pleasure all wrapped into one.

"Yes," I whisper unsure if the word actually left my body. I rock my hips up from the bed, trying desperately to keep up to his rhythm. He's fucking me hard and fast. The bed moves slightly with each tender assault. He's so strong, so muscular and he's so lost in our pleasure.

"Alexa, your body…." The words transform into a deep and animalistic grunt. "Fuck your body."

I grab hold of his shoulders trying to breathe. I'm so close again already. This feels so good. I can't tell him how good. No man has been so deep within every part of me before.

"Ah, fuck." He pulls back and takes my body with him, pulling me onto his lap as he pounds his cock effortlessly into my body.

"Your fucking pussy wants this." The words are pure and raw and only spur me on more. "You love this, don't you?"

I can't talk. It's all too much. I can only nod and rock against him.

"I'm going to come." He screams the words and his neck tenses, his shoulders stop and his hips pump over and over into me again.

Chapter 17

"Where will the show be?" I ask quietly as I finish dressing. I can't believe that just happened. I can't believe I can walk after that just happened. After tying up the condom, Noah had gone to get a warm cloth and had washed my body tenderly, wiping away all the sweat that had gathered on my chest and forehead before he pulled the wet, moist cloth between my folds. It was tender, too tender for the man who now sat in front of me, half-dressed staring at his smart phone.

"The show?" His eyes dart up and over my face before a small grin pulls at the corner of his lips. "My show?"

"The pictures you've been taking of me..." I suddenly feel embarrassed that others will see what he's been seeing. "Those pictures. Where will you be showing them?"

"In New York." He moves past me to retrieve a pad and paper from a desk in the corner of his bedroom. "I'll write down the details."

"I'm not sure I'll go." I feel way too connected to him to let this continue beyond our photography sessions. Logically I know most of that is tied in to everything that happened in Paris. I just had rebound sex with the best lover I've ever had. Why did he have to appear in my life right now? I wish I had met him before I'd left on my trip. Maybe if I'd never met Beck, my heart wouldn't feel as completely muddled as it does right now. I never had trouble separating lust from love but since I found out what love actually feels like a few months ago, the line between them is blurred beyond any recognition.

"Alexa." He pats the bed next to him. "Sit down."

I fidget in place, moving back and forth between my feet. I don't want to sit down. I've never felt this vulnerable before and I don't like it. I want to wash it away. As soon as I walk out of his front door, I'm jumping in a taxi and sprinting home to shower. Washing Noah Foster out of my body and mind can't be that hard, can it?

"Sit down." His tone is unyielding and commanding.

"Please don't take pictures of me right now," I say in a hushed tone. I can't handle that. The thought of him pulling out a camera so he can capture the post orgasmic glow on my face is more than I can shoulder right now.

"Sit," he repeats even louder than the last time.

I acquiesce and sit a few inches from him. My eyes settle on his hands and the piece of paper that is now dangling from his fingers.

"Here are the details." He shoves the paper onto my lap and I grab for it before it flutters to the floor. "Come to the show with me."

"What?" I glance at his face. I need confirmation of what he just asked me.

"Let's go to New York together."

A ball of desire pools within me. He wants to take me to New York, to his show. He never leaves his home and he wants us to travel to the city together.

"I thought…" I stammer as I search for the compassionate way to present what I need and want to say to him. "I thought you didn't go out."

"I don't." His eyes watch my face for any reaction. "I want to go with you."

"Why?" I shake my head wishing I had tempered that with more compassion. It's too direct.

"You make me feel safe." The words are soft and barely audible. Before I have time to respond, he's on his feet, his thumb scanning his phone signaling that the discussion is over.

Chapter 18

"The Brighton Beck is coming to town." The exuberance in Sadie's voice is unmistakable. It's the same giddiness that was there when she first talked about Noah. I can't say I'm shocked given the fact that she's been a Brighton Beck fan girl forever. The only difference now is that she has absolutely no idea that the world renowned watercolor artist is actually the same man I was sleeping with when I lived in Paris.

I can't react genuinely. If I do that she's going to stare down her nose at me for hooking up with him. "You're excited." That's a great comeback, Alexa. Now if you can just quiet the pounding of your heart to a dull roar, you might get through this conversation without confessing everything to your best friend. When I agreed to pop by to have a coffee with Sadie at the restaurant, I had no idea that Beck would be the sole focus of our visit.

"You remember him, don't you?" She asks as she pulls the plate of cookies across the table. "He was the friend that Hunter put you in touch with in Paris. Did you ever end up calling him?"

I'd called him days after I got his number when I was lost. He'd walked me through the maze of unfamiliar streets to a park bench where he and his incredibly handsome face had been waiting for me. I wasn't initially impressed with his talent, but his kindness, the tenderness he showed me as a lover and his profession of love for me had swept me off my feet. The fact that we were two Americans caught up in the romance of the city of lights didn't hurt either. We had an instant bond that cemented us together for weeks.

"Hunter's best friend, Jax, and his wife just had a baby. Brighton's coming to see them." Sadie's so sweet and unaware of the darkness that pervades Brighton's soul. To her, he's simply the brother of her husband's best friend. To the world he's a hero who whisked his girlfriend away to the best long term care facility in Europe after a horrific accident that left her unable to move. To me, he's the one man who managed to not only own my heart but also break it into five million unfixable pieces.

"They live in New York, right?" I want clarification of where he's going to be. I can't imagine that Beck would try and contact me while he's on US soil after everything that happened between us, but he's unpredictable and if I'm going to have to face him, I want at least some semblance of a warning bell so I could throw my defense into action.

She nods as she takes another bite of cookie. "I think he's coming to Boston too." She shrugs her shoulders. "Hunter didn't say why, but I hope he stops by here."

I hope he gets hit by a train. "I know you love his work," I offer. I need to find a way to change the subject. Even though I was under the spell of Brighton's lies when I slept with him, the cruel and unmistakable fact is that he was involved with someone else when we had our affair. I thought he was over her, but he was just as invested in his girlfriend Liz then, as he is now.

"I'll call you to come in and meet him if he books a table."

"That's okay." I reach over to pat her hand before standing to leave. "I'm not a fan."

Chapter 19

"Alexa. Christ. Let me come in your mouth." Noah's voice calls from above me as his hands pull hard on my hair. "Suck my cock."

I don't need the encouragement. I need an escape from my life. Sucking on Noah's dick was working. There was absolutely no way I could focus on anything but this right now.

"I'm going to shoot down your throat." His voice is deep, heavy and filled with measured desire.
I reach for his heavy balls, pulling them into my palm, kneading them as I suck heartily on the head of his dick. "Come," I whisper around the heavy root. Come so you can pound the memory of Brighton Beck right out of my body.

He rewards me with a burst of hot desire that lands right at the back of my tongue. I pull him out slowly, knowing from experience that with a man this big, it's going to be much more than I can handle in one swallow. I'm right. He pumps into me, over and over again, the thick hot stream pouring down my throat.

"Give me five minutes and I'll make you come." He leans back onto the mattress now as I still rest on my knees on the floor at the edge of his bed. "I have to catch my breath. Fuck, you suck cock better than…" he catches himself before anything else pops out of his mouth.

The almost comparison to another woman tears right through me. I rest my forehead against the sheet to temper my emotions. This isn't heavy. It's not serious. Don't take the shit he says to heart, Alexa. Don't let Brighton's asshole cheating ways ruin this for you.

"Alexa." Noah's voice cuts through my thoughts. "Look at me."

My head pops up and the end of the camera lens greets me. I hear the light tap of the shutter as he captures a steady stream of images of my face. "Noah," I whisper in mild protest.

"I'm going to say something to you…" he begins before he stops himself. "No." He pulls on my hands as a silent request to join him on the bed. I acquiesce and crawl into his lap, his cock resting heavily on the sheet between his open legs.

"What?" I trail a path along the large tattoo on his shoulder with my finger. I study all his tattoos each and every time I set eyes on him but whenever I've asked what each design represents, he changes the subject. It's obvious that the art that adorns his body is personal, too personal to share with me.

"We're done today." The words are clipped, direct and final.

"I know." I look in his eyes, wondering if he feels the same sense of loss that I do knowing that I don't have a reason to come back to his apartment after today.

His hands circle my body pulling me closer to him. "The work part is done," he clarifies. "The us part…do you want that to be done?"

Is he honestly asking me if I want to give him up? "You don't want it to be done?" I haven't considered that anything between us would last beyond our photo sessions. I was a temporary distraction in his life and he was the same to me. It started out that way at least. Has it changed?

"Something happened." He sits up straighter adjusting my weight in his lap. "You know I use an agency to find women to fuck, right?"

It's a raw confession that doesn't shock me at all. I do know that. I assume that he has on the number on speed dial and that he requests the company of women on a very regular basis. I don't have any ridiculous fantasy that he'd ever come out of his structured, very safe cocoon for me or anyone else for that matter.

"Women with fake accents," I correct him as I glide my hand to the tattoo on his chest.

"I called for one a few days ago."

My stomach drops into free fall mode even though I know that it's his reality. Why is there a hint of pain attached to the words when they come out of his mouth? Why does the confirmation of it hold more meaning than just the abstract knowledge of it?

"I couldn't fuck her." The chuckle that skirts the statement vibrates through his chest and into my body. "I actually told her that I needed to call her Alexa."

"You what?" I stifle my own giggle at the thought of him suggesting that to any woman.

"I was aching for you." I feel his cock spring to life beneath me. "It was the day after I fucked you. I thought if I fucked another woman, I'd wash it all away."

"Wash what away?" I know the answer. Ironically, it's exactly what I've been trying to do with Brighton.

"The need to have it again." His hand runs over my thigh and dives between my legs. "This again."

"You want to fuck me again?" I slide deeper into his embrace.

"And again and again." His lips skirt over my bare shoulder. "I'm not going to stop fucking you. I promise you that."

It's a promise that I'm counting on. Maybe Noah Foster wasn't my rebound fuck. Maybe he is where I'm supposed to be all along.

Chapter 20

"Why are you going to New York?" Sadie stares at me as I try to cram yet another dress into my overnight bag. "You're just taking off without any explanation."

"I'm meeting a friend there." It's not entirely a lie. Noah had suggested that we travel separately. I tried to coax him into taking the train with me, but he shied away from the idea quickly. So it was going to be me, my overnight bag and a pile of magazines for the long ride from Boston to New York this afternoon.

"Do I know this friend?" Her brow cocks with the question. "Is it a boy or a girl?"

"Boy or girl?" I parrot back. "You spend way too much time with toddlers."

"Cory is smarter than most adults I know." Sadie's smile broadens at the mention of her four-year-old stepson's name. "If I had more details about this mystery trip you're taking, I might want to tag along."

"You need a break from the old ball and chain that is Hunter," I say jokingly. "I can't imagine what it's like being married to that man."

"It's heaven." She literally almost swoons.

I love how happy she is. I've secretly wished for my own happily-ever-after since I flew back from Paris four months ago to watch her and Hunter exchange vows. It was a simple, elegant wedding with just a few select friends. When I left Boston to jet back to Paris it was with a longing for a romance like Sadie's. Maybe that's why it was so easy for me to fall into Brighton's arms and bed. I want to be loved the same way she is.

"Did you pack enough condoms?" The sweet, innocent tone of her voice doesn't match the vulgarity of the question.

"Did you just ask me about condoms?" I rock back on my heels with laughter. "You're fucking hilarious, Sadie." The last statement is meant to sound facetious in a good way.

"No one fucks as much as you do, Alexa." The thin grin that she's trying unsuccessfully to hold over her lips is giving away her true intentions. "You better bring a few boxes with you."

"I'm staying one night." I hold up my index finger to reiterate the declaration. "Just one night."

"Two boxes should do then."

***

I'll meet you at the show. I'm running late.

I read the text message Noah sent me for the third time. My stomach flops at the words. I've been fearful since we planned this adventure that he would bail on me. I know that he hates leaving the sanctity of his apartment.

Please hurry. I don't want to see my naked ass alone.

I smile as I send the message back to him. I've already showered and dressed in the elegant hotel room that Noah had arranged for me. The last time I was in the city was with Sadie and we had stayed at a nice place, but this trumped that tenfold. The champagne that had awaited my arrival sat chilling and still unopened. I didn't want to pop the cork until I was back in this room, naked with Noah toasting to his brilliance.

I glance at the clock on my phone and realize that the doors to the gallery will be opening within the hour. It won't hurt for me to go there now, and stand across the street to watch all the people filing in. It's also going to afford me the luxury of seeing Noah arrive. He's wearing a tuxedo. Since I've rarely seen him in clothing all, I'm looking forward to the image of that more than anything else.

I pick up my phone, toss it into my clutch, and take one last look at myself in the elegant, understated black dress I chose for the evening and slip out the door.

Chapter 21

"Champagne?" A stilted voice asks from my left.

I turn quickly to the image of a waiter, dressed impeccably with a silver tray resting on his palm. "Would you care for a glass of champagne?"

I pull one from the tray and nod a silent thank you to him. I down almost the entire glass in one swallow. It's more to temper my growing anxiety than to calm my anger. The show officially opened more than an hour ago and Noah has yet to appear. The canvases are all covered in creased, white sheets awaiting the unveiling which isn't going to happen until Noah makes his grand entrance.

"Is this your first time at a Noah Foster show?" A strong male voice asks from behind me.

I turn and I'm instantly greeted with the handsome face of an older gentleman. His hand darts out to take mine. "I'm Ron."

"Alexa." I smile back as I press my palm into his. "It's my first time."

"You're in for a treat." The way he cocks his brow is a little too playful. The old Alexa, the one pre-Paris, would have flirted shamelessly with him. Any and all male attention fed my unending need back then. Tonight, I want the focus to be on anyone but me.

"I can't wait," I offer in a lie that is strategically woven into a smile. "Does he always do this type of elaborate unveiling?"

"Always." He nods. "Noah Foster never shies away from putting on a spectacular show."

The words feel foreign to me. Noah likes to put on a show? That doesn't fall into the realm of the Noah I know. That Noah hides within the walls of his apartment.

I scan the room again searching in futile haste for Noah's face. I'm instantly aware of how many women are in the space. They're all blonde, blue eyed and about the same height as I am. Not one of them is attached to the arm of a man.

"Are you part of the show?" This time it's a woman's voice who invades my thoughts.

I signed a non-disclosure agreement and the consequence of breaking that is an amount of money that I can't hope to earn in my entire teaching career. "No," I lie effortlessly. "I'm just here to see."

She studies my face with elegant grace. Her hair bobs lightly as she twists her neck towards the door. "He's always late for these things."

"Are you part of the show?" I wonder aloud. The way she's dressed and the diamond pendant floating around her neck suggests she can pay any fine that Noah might dish out.

"Not this show." She pulls a weak grin across her lips. "Last year's show."

I soak in her appearance. She's brunette, her eyes a rich golden brown. She's slightly older than me, but her beauty is unmistakable. I can't help but wonder whether her experience with Noah mirrored mine.

"Attention." I recognize the man's voice calling to the room as Ron's. "Noah has arrived."

The crowd bursts into a raucous round of applause as my eyes dart around the room, searching for the one familiar face I long to see.

My gaze is pulled back to the front of the gallery and Noah's tall frame encased in a perfectly, tailored tuxedo. I try to get his attention, my hand flying helplessly in the air, but his focus isn't on me, it's on all the adoring patrons of his show who are eager to see the unveiling of the images of my naked body.

The space is so small. I feel trapped within a promise that I made weeks ago. Sharing my body with Noah had been one thing, but now, I'm about to see it in all its bare glory on four foot tall canvases.

"I want to thank each of you for coming." Noah's smooth and deep voice fills the cramped space. "I have a special guest I'd like to introduce you all to before we unveil the collection."

My heart pounds. He's going to call me up there and then everyone will know that the body he's been photographing for the past few weeks is mine.

"He's my hero." The fondness in the words is unmistakable. "I've admired his work for many, many years and he's one of my dearest friends."

I pull my body to the left as I try and catch a glimpse of Noah through the gathering crowd. I'm relieved by the knowledge that his special guest isn't actually me, after all. Maybe I can escape this evening with my anonymity still in place.

"I'm thrilled that Brighton Beck is here to help me introduce my newest collection. This is Desire."

My stomach recoils at the sight of Brighton hugging Noah. The sheets drop, spotlights fall on each of the twelve canvases and my world collapses beneath my trembling feet.

My eyes scan the images as my heart fights to keep beating.

Each canvas is a different woman.

All blonde.

All nude.

All sprawled out on the same bed in Noah's apartment.

Each face raw with wanton desire.

Including my own.

VAIN

PART TWO

Chapter 1

"I'd recognize your beautiful face anywhere."

I'd recognize that voice anywhere. It's the same voice that whispered into my ear during those nights in Paris when I was tucked into my bed, and his arms. It's the same voice that has left me countless voicemails since, asking me to talk, begging me for forgiveness. It's Brighton's voice.

"Beck." I feel a flash of pain sail through my body as his name hovers against my lips. This is the point where I'm supposed to turn around and face him but I can't pull my eyes from the canvas where my nude body is mocking me. Beck's presence is only adding an extra layer of humiliation to that. What vortex in the universe did I fall through where my past biggest mistake collides with my present worse mistake?

His hand catches my wrist and before I have a chance to recoil, his lips are brushing against my palm. "Alexa, I can't believe you're here."

I can't believe it either. I can't believe I have to deal with the man who told me he loved me while he was in a relationship with another woman. I can't do this right now. I need to find a gas can and a match so I can set my portrait on fire. That or I need to move to another country where no one knows my name, or face, or now, my breasts and half my ass.

"What are you doing here, Alexa?" Despite the fact that I'm literally almost ripping his hand from his arm trying to dislodge my wrist, he's not letting go. "Did you hear that I'd be here?"

My chest expands with a deep breath. The arrogance that seeps from beneath the question is one of the reasons I was initially attracted to him. Of course he'd assume I tracked him down. Why wouldn't he? I practically threw myself at his feet every chance I had while we were in Paris. "No." That's all I can find within me to say. What else is there?

"Then why are you here?" His eyes dart across the span of canvases, stopping briefly to study each one.

"It doesn't matter." It doesn't at this point.

"Do you know Noah Foster?"

I sigh, knowing that I should reconcile with the inevitable and tell Brighton how I ended up as the subject of one of Noah's portraits. I don't have enough spare emotional energy to do that right now. I have one mission, and one mission only, and that's to somehow rewind time so my naked body isn't part of this display of tits and ass.

"Where's Noah?" I find the words, pushing them together into a barely audible question.

Brighton shifts his body so he's standing directly in front of me now. His head bobs into my field of view and I pull my gaze from my portrait long enough to glance at his face. It's the devastatingly handsome face that I fell in love with only a few months ago. His brown hair is slightly longer now but that's the only difference. He looks exactly as I remember him. "Alexa, you're white as a ghost."

"Where's Noah?" I repeat the question, my voice rising enough that several people next to us, turn abruptly to look.

His hand squeezes my wrist before it slides down to cup my hand. "What's wrong?"

The question demands a simple answer. He's expecting me to say that I'm overwhelmed with seeing him and perhaps, in some small way, I am. I'd imagined this moment in time, when I came face-to-face with Brighton again, a million times over in my mind and not once was it while a portrait of my naked body was hanging in the same room. "I need to talk to Noah."

He cocks his head to the side, his eyes scurrying over my expression before darting behind me. "He's busy with a buyer." The words are clipped, direct and steady.

"A buyer?" Fuck me. I can't let anyone buy that portrait. I need to take it before it ends up in office of some overly wealthy, older gentlemen who uses it to spur on his libido.

"What's going on with you and Noah?" he asks in a hush.

I shake my head limply from side-to-side. "I don't know." I don't know. I delivered a sandwich as a favor weeks ago and now I'm standing here, looking into the eyes of the only man I've ever loved while my entire future is being stolen from me by Noah Foster.

His head darts back to look at the portraits and I feel a blush course though me. He's seen me exactly as I am on the large canvas.

He's touched every place that is now there for everyone to see, yet I feel more exposed than I did when we were making love. "Can we go somewhere to talk?"

"I can't leave." My hand flits past his face towards the canvas. "I need to take care of that."

"What?" His blue eyes squint together as he thoroughly studies my expression. "What are you talking about?"

I want to break open and grab hold of Brighton to steady myself. He was my anchor when I felt adrift in Paris. Since I saw him cuddling his girlfriend in the café down the street from my flat, I've convinced myself that the only reason I fell so hard and so fast for him was the fact that he offered me stability in a world that was literally, completely foreign to me. Now I'm in the most vulnerable place I've ever been and his voice holds the same tender composure it did during all those long nights in my bed when I gave my heart and body to him.

"I need to talk to Noah." I jar my wrist free of Brighton's grip and turn sharply. I need to deal with him. I know that I do, but not tonight. Tonight my wrath is honed in one direction and that's straight at Noah.

"Alexa, wait," he says, his hand briefly skims over my waist before I dart into the crowd. I scan the faces, noting immediately how many of them mirror my own. The blonde, blue eyed women punctuating the otherwise male gathering all resemble me in a restrained way. Our features are different, but our bodies are so strikingly similar. They're the other models. I see quiet composure on their faces now, but the desire that screams from the photographs can't mask their identities. It can't mask mine either and if Noah sells that portrait, everything I've worked for is going to be sacrificed because he couldn't keep a promise.

I spot Noah in deep conversation with the man I briefly spoke with before the unveiling. It's Ron, the older gentlemen who told me that Noah likes to put on a show. He wasn't kidding. I march up to them, my anger only being tempered by the fact that I just saw Brighton, and the shock of that has sucked up the majority of my emotional energy.

"That man over there is staring at my breasts."

"Do you blame him?" Noah nods towards my chest. "That's quite the dress."

"I'm not talking about my dress." My eyes dart down to where my breasts are spilling out of the top of the simple black dress I chose for the occasion. I wish I hadn't picked something so low cut. I feel exposed enough as it is after seeing the unveiling of my nude portrait in all its glory and coming face-to-face with Brighton.

"What are you talking about then?" His eyes shoot behind me to the crowd milling around the portraits. It's obvious from the grin on his face that he's enjoying all the attention his work is getting.

"My portrait." I skim my hand through the air to the left and the line of photographs everyone else in the room is gathered around. "That man right there is staring at mine. He's been locked to that spot for the past five minutes."

Ron's brows shoot up before he murmurs something about getting a drink. He dashes into the crowd giving me the much needed privacy to talk with Noah that I've been craving.

Noah's eyes narrow as his gaze falls to me. "Alexa, that's not you in the portrait."

My stomach flips and I feel as though everything in it is going to come racing out. What kind of game is he trying to play with me? "What? Noah, don't lie to me. Don't do that."

"Do what?" His hands reach to grab my shoulders. "It's not you."

"It's me." I cling to his eyes with my own, searching the depth of his for some understanding. He promised me that he wouldn't display my face and he betrayed me. Even after everything we shared together in his bed, he stabbed me in the back. My entire life's course is going to change from this moment forward because of him.

"Come with me." His voice is soft as he sweeps my hand into his. "This way."

Chapter 2

"I can't look at it, Noah." My throat is so dry I have to swallow before I can get the words out. "Just take it away."

"Alexa." His hands are in the pockets of his pants, his head bowed down towards mine. "Turn your head and look at it."

The mumblings of the people around us isn't helping. Any nerve that I had when I was twenty feet away from the portrait has now dissolved into the vapor. It's right there. It's so close I can touch the canvas. I can't turn my head to look at it. My gaze is steady, and set, on Noah's face.

"Noah." A woman's voice carries over my shoulder. "I've been trying to catch you all night. Can we talk?"

His eyes jump from my face to hers and then back to mine. "I'm busy, Ari. Not now."

"I came tonight because of you." She slides into my field of view. It's the same brunette that I exchanged empty pleasantries with earlier. She was one of last year's models, perhaps both literally and figuratively. The way her gaze bites into me suggests that she wants him. Her body language is screaming it.

"I'm busy." His hand reaches for mine.

Her eyes follow the movement of his arm and her shoulders tense. "It's important, Noah. I just need five minutes."

His body shifts slightly and I feel his index finger slide over my chin pulling my eyes back to his. "Ari, this is more important. If you'll excuse us…"

"If you don't talk to me now, Noah, I'm leaving," she snaps.

"Goodbye, Arianna." His deep voice is measured and restrained. His stare pierces through me.

"Fuck you," she hisses as she turns on her heel.

He doesn't flinch as his hand slides across my chin until he's cupping it firmly in his grasp. I don't try and move as his lips brush mine. "Look at the portrait, Alexa," he whispers into my mouth. "Look at it."

"I can't," I mumble. "Please don't make me. I'm so embarrassed."

His lips trail a heated path across my cheek to my ear. "The woman in this portrait isn't you. She's not as beautiful as you."

I pull back and scan his eyes. "It's me."

I don't resist as he pulls my back into his chest and turns us both towards the portrait. My eyes shut briefly knowing that when I open them, I'll have to face the choice I made weeks ago when he asked me to model for him. I'll have to take responsibility for trusting a man I didn't know. A man I knew was immersed in a world I'd never fully understand.

"Open your eyes." His warm breath skirts over my shoulder. I feel his hand snake around my waist, pulling my body into his. "You expected to see yourself in the photographs. This woman is ordinary. She's nothing like you."

I lean forward, wanting to distance myself from the desire that I can't temper. It's unwanted and misplaced, but it's there. The touch of his body against mine, the hint of his arousal pressing into me and the scent of his skin is threatening my better judgment. I slowly open my eyes.

"See the curve of her shoulder." His lips brush against the bare skin of my shoulder. "It's not as soft as yours."

I study the portrait, unable and unwilling to see what he sees. "It's my shoulder."

"Look at her hip." He reaches forward, his fingers running along the portrait. "It's not as broad as yours. She can't use her body the same way you do. Your body was made to take pleasure." His hand jumps to my hip, pulling a slow path across it.

I shake my head without thinking from side-to-side. "No," I whisper. "That's me."

"Her nipples." His hand winds up the front of my dress until it's cupping the underside of my left breast. "Her nipples are small. See how swollen they are." I feel the nod of his chin against my cheek. "Your nipples are full and plump."

"Noah," I whisper as I feel him pull my body closer to his. His finger lazily courses over the fabric to rub against my growing nipple. It's so brazen. There are people standing within feet of us, but there's no uncertainty in his movements at all.

"Look at her face, Alexa." His hand jumps to my chin. "Your face is so much more beautiful."

"It's my face." I tilt my head to the left, trying to find the familiarity I did earlier when I first saw the portrait across the room.

"She looks like you." His lips touch my cheek as he whispers into my skin, "she's not perfect like you."

I stare at the portrait, soaking in all the fine details of the woman's profile. The long blonde hair, the sculpted brow, and the full lashes. They all look like me. "It looks like me," I repeat back to him.

"It's not you." He leans closer, his breath skirting over my ear. "I couldn't show your photographs tonight."

I turn around, my mind still a mass of confusion. "Why?"

He holds my gaze as he takes a steady breath before he speaks, "I want those for myself. They're only for my eyes."

I need a reprieve from the serious undertone of the response. I can't ask him what he means. If I do that, I'm going to open a door I'm not certain I want to walk through yet. I flip back around and study the portrait again. I still see glimpses of myself within it. It looks too much like me. If I see it, others will too. "It looks so much like me. You just changed something with software on your computer. It's still me. "

"She's here." He pulls his hands away from my body. "I'll go get the model and then you'll see for yourself it's not you."

I don't move. I can't.

Chapter 3

"You look like me." The pitch of her voice is higher than mine, there's a Southern lilt within it that she's trying to mask. I can tell by the way she speaks in an even tone. "You really look like me."

I stare at her face. She could be my sister. She's slightly more petite than I am, but her features resemble mine. "You do look like me."

"No, you look like me," she teases as she runs her fingers along my forearm. "I love your shoes."

I look down at the plain, black stilettos I chose for the evening. My desire to mute my appearance so I could fade into the background once my pictures were revealed has been blown to hell. I've created my own circle of attention because I assumed the portrait was me. Why wouldn't I? Noah took my photograph for weeks for this show.

"Do you like my picture?" Her hand gracefully runs over the length of her body on the canvas.

"It's beautiful," I whisper as my eyes glide over it with an awakened perspective. I see her within the lines of the woman's face now. I see how her lips jut forth when she opens her mouth. I see the contour of her brow. I see her lost in pleasure. The pleasure that she felt when she was in Noah's bed.

"I didn't think I could look like that." There's vulnerability woven within the words. "Men told me I was pretty when I… you know…when they hired me."

"You're really beautiful," I say the words deliberately. She is.

"You're saying that because we look so much alike." The weakness washes away and a dazzling smile covers her lips.

I can't help but smile back, even though a part of my mind is locked on the image of Noah pulling his body from hers before he reached for his camera to capture the flush that had raced over her face and body after she came.

"I'm glad you two met." There's marked amusement in Noah's voice.

"You definitely have a type," she quips playfully before grabbing his hand in her own.

He jerks back suddenly and my eyes dart to his face. It's locked on something behind me. A wide grin covers his mouth and he inches forward. "Here's someone you both should meet."

"What have we here?" Brighton's voice does little to soothe all the confusion I'm feeling. He's caught up to me. I can feel him behind me. I thought I'd dodged that bullet for the night when I disappeared into the crowd.

I don't respond. I'm not emotionally mature enough to be able to separate everything I'm feeling to the point where I can deal with Brighton objectively. I'm feeling so scattered right now that I'm tempted to rush out the door with him. I know that falling back into his arms will wash away Noah's words from my body and the unwanted knowledge that he probably fucked each of the twelve women in these photographs.

"I'm Amy." The model in Noah's portrait thrusts her arm out. I feel the friction against my arm when she shakes Brighton's hand.

"Brighton," he acknowledges in a warm tone.

"I need to mingle." Her hand brushes against my shoulder. "We can party later."

"No, I…" my voice trails wishing I could somehow communicate to her that I don't want her to walk away. The moment she does that, I'm going to be alone with these two.

"The four of us." She twirls her perfectly manicured hand in the air, circling it around Noah, Brighton and I. "I'm working out of a hotel down the street tonight. Noah, you game? I'll cut you a special rate."

I flinch when I feel Brighton's hand rest on my hip. I try to step forward but he clamps down, holding me in place. His hot breath runs over my shoulder.

Noah's eyes blaze over Brighton before settling on his hand. "Brighton, you just met her. Hands off." His tone is meant to be teasing and playful but there's a fierceness that skirts the edge.

Amy's eyes follow the path of Noah's gaze and her brows rise. "He wants her which means you're stuck with me."

"We're done here, Amy." He reaches down to run his lips over her cheek. "You can go."

"We'll party later?"

"No. We won't." He pulls back from her, his jaw set and rigid.

She shrugs her shoulders, takes one last longing look at her nude portrait and turns towards the crowd. She flawlessly glides into place beside an older man, her arm comfortably lacing around his shoulder.

"Brighton, your hand." Noah's chin drops as his eyes focus once again on Brighton's unyielding grip on my hip.

"Alexa was upset earlier." Brighton steps closer until his body is pressed firmly against mine. "I'm just checking on her."

Noah's jaw tightens as his eyes dart from my face to Brighton's. "She's fine. It's been a long day. I'm taking her back to our room."

"Your room?" Brighton hisses. "You're staying in a room with him?"

"She's with me," Noah growls. The words don't hold any ambiguity. They're direct and concrete.

"Beck." I exhale in a heated rush. "I didn't have a chance to tell you..."

"Beck?" Noah sucks in a deep and measured breath. "Why did you call him that? What the hell is going on, Alexa?"

This is the first, and only time, I've seen the impassable façade of Noah Foster, the famed photographer, crack. He takes a heavy step forward and I recoil just from the sheer mass of his large frame. I feel my knees buckle and Brighton's hands surround my waist to offer me stability. I reach for one, not as a gesture of gratitude, but as a point of balance. Noah's penetrating gaze burns a path to where my hand now covers Brighton's, holding steadfast to it.

"You know each other?" His mouth twitches as the words sail over his lips. "How? From where?"

The stiff silence that fills the air behind me shouldn't surprise me. It's not as though Brighton will pipe up and explain that he was sleeping with me while tending to the needs of his injured girlfriend in Paris. I drop my hand from his as I take a small step towards Noah. The air in the slender space between them is heavy and thick with confusion.

"It doesn't matter." I mean it. It doesn't matter at this point how I know Brighton or where we met. "It doesn't matter anymore."

"Tell me how you know each other." Noah's posture stiffens, his hands bolt to his hips. "Brighton, how do you know her?"

"I lived in Paris for a semester," I stall, wanting to find the right words to explain this to him. "We have mutual friends."

His breath shoots over my forehead. "How well do you know him?"

"Noah," I whisper, wanting to temper my confession. I have no idea if he knows Brighton's girlfriend, Liz. I don't know if Brighton is still with her. I can barely shoulder the guilt of having an affair with him. How can I tell Noah about that when they're such close friends?

His hands jump to my face, cupping both my cheeks. He leans down, resting his forehead against mine. "Alexa," he whispers into the air between us. "Tell me."

"I can't." I jerk back hoping that Brighton will take the lead and fill in the blanks for Noah. Again, only muted silence fills the space behind me. "He was there with his girlfriend. I didn't know. I wouldn't have done it if I knew about her."

Noah's eyes pierce into me, his expression stoic. "You've fucked him, haven't you?"

I can only hang my head in shame. I hear a muted curse as he brushes past me and his footsteps disappear into the hum of the crowded gallery.

Chapter 4

"I saw Beck." I lean back on the couch, shifting my legs so my feet are resting against the edge of the small table.

"Beck?" Kayla shrieks from the kitchen." You're shitting me."

"I'm not," I begin. "It was three days ago. I went to New York for a thing and he was there." *A thing?* I can't come up with something better than that. It's not surprising given the fact that I've blocked out much of that trip out of sheer need. I'd waited in that empty hotel room all night for Noah to arrive and he hadn't. The long and lonely train ride home had given me ample time to decide that I needed to put Noah Foster and Brighton Beck behind me. One had abandoned me in the heart of New York City and the other had broken my heart in the most romantic city in the world. I need to stay away from anyone who makes their living selling art.

"What kind of thing?" She bounces towards me with a full plate of nachos in her hand.

"Where did you get the cheese for that?" I lean forward, my nose inhaling the scent wafting from the plate. "I haven't bought any cheese in a long time."

"I cut off the green parts." She shrugs her shoulders as she tosses a crunchy chip into her mouth. "Try them. They're good."

"I'll pass." I push the plate back at her. "I'm not that brave."

"What did he say to you?" I can barely make out her words between the bites.

"We didn't have a chance to talk." It wasn't a lie. We hadn't. The fact that Brighton had sent several text messages since I saw him in New York isn't worth mentioning to Kayla. Knowing her, and her insatiable need for all things romantic, she'd want me to call him up and arrange a dinner date right now. I'd managed to lose Brighton again in the gallery right after Noah walked away. I had no intention of talking to him now, or ever. Seeing him again had been the reminder I needed. The reminder that I fucked around with a man in a committed relationship was in the forefront of my brain. I was never going to go down that painful road again.

"What was it like?" She takes another bite of a chip and then shakes her head. "Maybe the cheese is bad."

I wrench the plate from her grasp and put it on the table. "We can go out for something to eat."

"You said you wanted to stay in."

I had said that. After getting back from a run an hour ago I felt the need to talk to someone. Kayla was the obvious choice. I still didn't have the courage to tell Sadie about any of this. She loved me, and worried about me too much not to get in the middle of it.

"I need to get a good night's sleep," I half lie. "Tomorrow I have an interview for a placement as a student teacher."

"What?" she shrieks as she jumps to her feet. "We should go out and celebrate."

I can't contain a laugh. "No, we shouldn't. I can't be hung over when I go in for my interview."

"This is it." She claps her hands together in genuine glee. "This is the last step and then you're going to be a real teacher."

I smile at the proclamation. This was the last step. One semester of teaching under the watchful eye of the teaching staff at the grade school nearby and I'd officially be a certified teacher.

***

"Where's my sandwich?" Noah's eyes tear a path over me. When Sadie had texted me as I was walking home from my job at the school, I'd fought with my own better judgment about whether or not to make the delivery. When I called her to tell her to let Bernie handle it, she told me Noah had called three times insisting I bring his food.

"Christ, Noah." My eyes dart from his groin to his face. "Put on some pants."

"It's not like you haven't seen it all before." His arm brushes past my arm to close the door behind me. "Where's my sandwich?"

"I gave it to the man who lives in the alley next to your building." I pull on the zipper of my sweater feeling a sudden need to cover the sheer white blouse I'm wearing. "You weren't going to eat it anyway."

A low chuckle races through his body. "You're right. I wasn't going to."

"Can you put on some pants?" I ask not only because it's way too distracting to look at his cock while I chastise him for leaving me alone in New York, but because it reminds me of those moments in his bedroom. Those are the moments that tug on my desire. I've come by my own hand countless times since I last saw him. The memory of him sliding his cock into me and racing his tongue over my folds is still right there. It always pulls my need to the surface at first thought.

He runs his tongue over his bottom lip as he stares at my face. "Don't run away. I'll be right back."

I bite my tongue to fight the urge to throw the words back in his face. He was the one who ran away in New York after discovering my connection to Brighton. He was the one who hadn't sent me a single text message in over a week. Come to think of it, he...

"Do you want something to drink?" He's back in the room, a pair of jeans now covering the bottom half of his body.

"No." I stand firmly in place. "Why didn't you just text me if you wanted to talk?"

He stops mid-step and shoves his hands into his pockets. "You bringing me a sandwich is our thing. I like that we have a thing."

My gaze rakes past him to the open concept apartment. I soak in the luxury of the space, using the time to consider my response. "I like it too," I offer quietly. I do like it. I like that he thinks of the first moment we laid eyes on each other.

"I thought you weren't coming." He turns towards the spacious living room. "I ordered that sandwich hours ago."

"I'm here now." I am, but maybe not for long. "What did you want to talk about?"

"Where to start," he chuckles as he pulls his hands together in front of him. "Let's talk about Brighton."

I follow the path he takes with my eyes, watching as he settles his tall frame onto his couch. He throws his arm over the back of it. I take it as a silent invitation to join him. I don't budge. My feet remain firmly planted in the black boots I'm wearing in his foyer.

"What about him?" I ask in a muted tone. I'm still unsure how much Noah knows about Brighton's relationship with his girlfriend.

"He told me about what happened between you two." He looks over his shoulder to where I'm standing.

I step back towards the door of his apartment, wanting to make a quick escape. Brighton has been hiding behind a veil of half-truths when it comes to our relationship. He's never acknowledged to me that he cheated on his girlfriend. Each time I'd confronted him about it on the phone after returning home, he'd told me it was complicated and that I wouldn't understand. His not-so-gentle reminders that I'm a decade younger than him have always stung, especially when he assumes I can't understand the basics of emotional connections. To Brighton, I'm the naïve, young girl who fell for the brilliant artist in Paris.

"Don't you want to know what he said?" He cocks a brow. The assumption beneath the gesture is glaringly obvious. He's testing me to see how invested I still am in Brighton.

"Beck has his own version of reality." My voice is a measure higher than my intention. I should expound on the answer and explain that Brighton had told me he wasn't with his girlfriend at the time. They're friends though and judging by Noah's glowing introduction of Brighton at his photography show's opening, Brighton's side of the story would hold much more weight than mine.

"Tell me your version of reality, Alexa."

Chapter 5

I feel like a caged animal that is about to get pushed to its limits by an aggressive, skillful handler. "It's in my past." I run my hand along my hip, pressing it into the soft denim of my jeans.

"It didn't look like it was your past when I saw you two together in New York."

Another woman might have given in to the overwhelming desire to snap back at him. He's trying to pull me into a web. A web where I'll confess to him that I love Brighton and that seeing him in New York has unhinged the deepest parts of my heart. "Noah." My foot taps hard against the wood floor. "What I had with Brighton ended when I left Paris. It was before I met you."

"He's one of my oldest friends." His mouth tightens. "He's also an asshole."

I watch as he pulls his tall lean body from the couch. He takes a step towards me. I want to agree with his declaration. Brighton is an asshole but looking at Noah's beautiful face, and seeing the pain within his eyes, makes me wish that Brighton Beck would just drop off the face of the earth.

"You don't have anything to add, Alexa?" He moves closer. "Tell me if you still want him."

I shake my head slightly from side-to-side as he narrows the gap between us. "I don't want him."

"He wants you."

"I don't want him," I repeat as he steps even closer. "I don't."

"You loved him." It's a declaration, not a question. "He told me you loved him."

"It feels like a lifetime ago." I take a step back, needing to separate my insatiable desire for his body from my need to stay level headed. "I fell in love with who I thought he was."

"Who do you think he is now?"

I take a shaky breath. "Someone who is bad for me. Someone who lied to me."

"What about me?" He crosses his arms across his broad chest. "Am I bad for you?"

I nod slowly. "You left me there alone. You abandoned me in New York City."

He rubs wearily at his forehead. "I had to calm down. The thought of his body inside of you," he hisses the words out through clenched teeth. "If I would have come to that hotel room, Alexa, I would have said things that hurt you. I would have lashed out at you."

"You didn't call or text to tell me what was going on." I pat my hand over my chest trying to slow my racing heartbeat. "I stayed awake all night waiting for you."

"He touched all of that." His chin bows as his eyes rake over my body. "He's tasted it. He's come inside of you." A thick vein pulses in his neck. "He owned that heart."

I push my hand against my chest wishing I could stall my heart for a beat. "Not any more. It was so long ago."

"I had to decompress." His hand jumps into the air before he pulls it into a tight fist. "I had to get away from Brighton and from you. I had to process it all."

"You made me feel like shit," I spit out. "You just took off."

"I had to." His gaze hardens. "I knew if I didn't, I'd fuck it up with you. I'd say things… things you'd never forgive me for."

"Things about how stupid I was in Paris?" I'm not looking for a verbal confirmation; I can see the agreement in his eyes.

He steps forward again, his muscular chest and arms on full display. "You and I are more alike than you realize, Alexa."

I feel the hard wooden door against my back and I realize I'm trapped in that web he's been weaving for me. "How so?" I pull my tongue across my bottom lip.

His left hand jumps to cup my cheek as his right hand falls to my hip. He's towering over me, his eyes so dark and haunting. "We both fell in love with the wrong person."

I nod, replaying in my mind the tender confession he made about loving a woman who was devoted to someone else. "We did," I whisper back, my eyes fixated on his mouth.

He sucks in a heavy breath before his mouth brushes over mine. My hands jump to his shoulders to gain balance. I reach out to deepen the kiss and he pulls me into his body. A deep, low growl pours from within him and into me. I feel my breasts swell beneath my heady desire. I didn't come here for this, but I can't stop it. I won't. I've never been so physically attracted to any man before. My sex clenches when he purrs my name into our kiss.

"Alexa," he whispers my name again, this time against my lips. "Let me help you forget him."

I wrap my fingers through his dark hair as I pull his mouth back onto mine.

***

"Ride my dick, Alexa. Ride it hard."

I push back against his legs as I drag my wetness over his lap, pulling his thick, swollen cock deeper within me. "Noah, yes," I whimper, my body clenching around him.

"You were made for fucking." His voice is thick and heavy with desire. "You're so wet. Your pussy is so tight."

The brash words only spur me on more. I drag my tits across his lips as I lean forward, pounding my body down onto his. I grab his strong shoulders using them to steady my balance as I fuck him hard. My body is bobbing above him while his cock strains within me.

"I'm going to fucking blow my load." He pulls my nipple into his mouth, the searing pain of his teeth bearing down on it coursing a hot path directly to my sex.

"Noah, that's so much," I cry out.

He licks the swollen, red bud and traces it with long, leisurely licks of his tongue. "Your tits are amazing."

"I'm so close." I squeeze my eyes shut. My body is already a quivering mess from when he lapped at my folds until I came all over his face on the floor by the door. Now that I'm sitting on his lap on the couch, I can't control my body. I want to fall over the edge again.

"Come for me." He bites out between clenched teeth. "Show me how good it feels."

I throw my head back and let the orgasm wash through me. I feel his hands circle my waist, pushing my hips down hard into him as he grinds his cock into the deepest parts of me. The bite of pain only adds to the rush and I cry out, screaming his name.

"Fuck, Alexa." His voice is dark and seductive. "Take everything I give you."

I still as he pumps his hips into me, filling the condom with his own sweet desire. My name sliding slowly between his lips as his eyes roll back in his head.

Chapter 6

"Do you want to go out for something to eat?" I zip up my sweater before pulling my boots back onto my feet.

He stares at me from where he's still seated on the couch, his long legs falling open, his cock still semi-erect. "No, I can order us something in."

"Not sandwiches," I tease.

"I hate sandwiches," he chuckles as he pulls himself up. "We could get a pizza?"

"Noah." I steel a breath before I continue, "I'd like to go out to eat."

The glint in his eye dims at the words. "I can't, Alexa."

I think for a brief moment about how to respond. "Why did you go to New York? There were a lot of people there."

He walks towards me, stopping briefly to pick up a wayward magazine that had fallen off the coffee table when he pushed against it, moving it out of our way as he carried me to the couch. "I know all those people."

"All of them?"

"They don't care about it." He doesn't expand on his response but I know the true meaning within the words.

"They don't care about your scar," I whisper back. "People won't care about it if we go out."

"I'll care about it," he snaps back as he brushes past me. "I'll get the take out menus. You can choose what we eat."

***

"I'm going to tell you something, Sadie, and you're not going to freak out." I glare at her across the table in Axel Boston. "Promise me you're going to hold it together."

She's on her feet in a flash, bouncing up and down as she jumps in joyful glee. "You're pregnant, aren't you? I can't wait to tell Hunter."

I roll my eyes and pat the edge of the table. "Sit back down. I'm not knocked up."

"What?" She slowly lowers herself back into the chair, the glint that was in her eyes just a moment before, now replaced with unmistakable disappointment. "I thought we were going to have a baby."

"That's a subject you need to bring up with Hunter's cock." I tip my chin towards her. "You two should get on top of that tonight. Or you could get on top. Or whatever the hell boring, old, married couples do when they get it on."

"I like it from behind."

"Gross, Sadie." I pull my hands to cover my ears. "Never tell me again what you and Hunter do in bed. TMI."
She pulls her hand to cover her mouth as she lets out a series of high pitched giggles. "If you're not pregnant, what then?"

"Promise first." I stick out my pinky finger, reverting back to when we were eight-years-old and would pinky swear. "Promise you're not going to go crazy when I tell you this."

She loops her small finger through mine and nods her chin. "I promise."

"I'm sleeping with Noah Foster." I blurt the words out in a frenzied rush.

"Oh that?" She leans back in her chair, placing her hands on her lap. "I thought you were."

"What?" I shake my head wondering if I'm hearing her right. "You knew?"

"He kept calling here asking for you to bring him a sandwich." She raises one brow, "Bernie told me Noah hates sandwiches and only orders them so he can chat with Bernie."

I sit in stunned silence. When did she figure it out and why the hell didn't she tell me she had? "Why didn't you say something?"

"Like what?" She shrugs. "He's a recluse. He probably made you sign something that says you can't talk about him. I read online that he does that."

"You read online that he makes his lovers sign things?" I parrot back, hoping that she doesn't see the truth within the words when I say them.

"Or his models." She sighs." Something like that. I'm just glad you're not one of them."

"One of who?" I ask, already knowing what her answer will be.

"At least you never modelled for him." She pushes her chair back from the table. "The last thing a teacher needs is naked pictures of herself floating around."

Chapter 7

"Why were those women's faces showing in the gallery photographs?" I take a sip of the coffee I brought with me to Noah's apartment. "You told me that you never take pictures of faces."

He pulls the plastic lid off his cup and blows on it. "I told you that I don't photograph faces. I don't." He takes a small taste from the cup. "I photograph women's bodies and sometimes a part of their face becomes vital to the story the image is telling."

"Your contract says you can't publically show any part of the woman's face," I push. That point has eaten at me since I saw the photographs on display in the gallery. I was horrified when I thought he broke our contract to show my face. He must have to deal with the legal and emotional ramifications of showing all those women's faces.

"No." The word is steady and clipped.

"No?" I repeat back. "I can show you my contract. It clearly says that." I know that fact without any reservation since I've read my contract repeatedly. Sadie's words about Noah photographing me have been haunting me. When we stop sleeping together he'll still own the rights to the pictures he took of me. I have to be certain that he can't ever show my face to anyone.

"Your contract says that," he corrects me. "The women in the gallery had a much different contract than you."

My chin lifts at the confession. "What? Why?"

He moves to place the paper cup onto the coffee table. "Do you remember the night we met?"

I nod my head while I examine his face waiting for him to continue.

"When you first got here I thought you were an escort." He rubs the back of his neck with his right hand, causing his bicep to flex. He's stunning. I have to put in effort to pull my gaze from his body back to his face.

"I remember," I chuckle. "You wanted to know how much."

"I had a contract ready that night. I always do when I call for a girl…" he stops himself, pulling his tongue across his bottom lip before he continues. "I always did when I called for a girl. I haven't called for one in weeks."

I take comfort in the tender confession. We've never spoken of the litany of call girls who have graced this apartment. I'm not naïve enough to believe that the one I crossed paths with during my first visit here, was the only one he called for. It was the way he satisfied his cravings. Up to this point, I hadn't wondered if it still was. I'd only assumed he'd given it up.

"I'd call for one and then wait for her to arrive." He pulls his palm across his bare leg. "If I thought she'd be perfect for one of my showings, I'd give her the contract and ask her to come back with it signed and notarized."

I take a sip of my coffee to try and mask my expression. He can see the question that's lingering behind my eyes. I know that he can.

"If I didn't think she'd work within my show, I'd fuck her." There's no hesitation in the words. They're clipped, direct and hurried.

"When I got here that night…" the question is there, waiting on my tongue but to form the words takes more courage than I have at this point.

"I wanted both so desperately." His fingers touch the tip of his growing erection.

I stare down at myself. My body still fully dressed in a pair of jeans and a black sweater. "You said we were going to fuck." The words sound needy and harsh. My sex clenches at the reminder of his declaration that night.

"When I opened the door and saw you, I knew I had to fuck you."

"What about those women in the gallery show?" I level my gaze at his face, trying not to look down at his crotch. "What about Amy?"

"What about them?" He leans back, his hand dropping to his cock, his fingers grazing over the tip.

"They all agreed to let you show their faces?" I press on, knowing if I don't ask the question right now, it's going to free fall between the cracks and I'll never get the answer I want. "Did you fuck any of them?"

He cocks a brow and bites his bottom lip. "Yes and no."

"Yes and no?"

"They all agreed to let me show their faces." He leans forward so his lips are hovering over mine. "No, I didn't fuck any of them."

I pull back, examining his expression. "They all look like they just fucked you in those pictures."

He tips his head forward a touch, a wide grin blazes across his lips and he whispers softly, "I didn't fuck any of them. I watched them touch themselves until they came. That's the moment I captured each and every time."

Chapter 8

"I need to get out more, Lex." Kayla rubs her hand across her forehead. "So you're screwing a photographer and he tells you that he watches hookers get off and then he takes their picture?"

"Technically, yes." I feel the need to qualify it." I mean he didn't tell me that when we were in the middle of having sex."

"How do you feel about it?" She moves the martini glass she's been drinking from for the past hour away from her on the bar. "I mean, how do you feel knowing he's watching hookers get off in his bed?"

It's eating me alive from the inside out. "I don't know," I say in a half lie. I know it was before Noah and I met. Wait. I assume it was. Maybe some of those photographs were taken after I showed up at his apartment. Maybe he'd been taking those pictures until the day before his New York show. I have no idea and the fact that I don't, that's what's ripping me apart. After he'd brazenly told me that the other night, I made an excuse about needing to grade papers and I took off. I didn't want to jump all over him about it knowing he'd likely tell me it was part of *his process.*

"What's the status with the two of you now?"

"We don't have a status." We don't. The only definition of our relationship that I can come up with is casual lovers.

"Are you going to tell him that it's bugging you out?" She runs her finger along the edge of the glass.

"I don't know." I shrug my shoulders. "He's kind of eccentric."

"How so?" The corner of her mouth pops up in a slight grin. "Does he wear socks to bed?"

"I've never seen him wear socks." I laugh. "He's almost always nude."

"Shut the fuck up." She bounces on the edge of her bar stool. "Is he hot?"

I have to close my eyes to temper my response. I pull in a breath to steady the sudden ache in my body. "He's the hottest guy I've ever met. Seriously hot, Kayla. Big, built and tattoos everywhere."

"Fuck me," she purrs. "It sounds like Beck has some serious competition."

"Beck?" I tap my finger across the bar. "Brighton Beck is no match for Noah Foster. No match in any way."

"Noah?" She leans forward, her eyes bright. "Noah Foster? Are you fucking the Noah Foster, the photographer who takes all those naked pictures?"

That non-disclosure agreement I signed just went to hell in a hand basket. "That's the one. I'm fucking the one and only Noah Foster."

***

"Now that you came down my throat I need to tell you something." I run my tongue over my lips, capturing the lingering taste of Noah's release.

"You sucked me off so you could confess some sin?" He leans back on his bed, his arms folded behind his head. "I seriously don't give a shit what it is. That was amazing."

I slide on top of him, rubbing my wetness against his stomach. "You're so handsome. I wish you could see what I see."

He smiles slightly at my words before he dips his cheek into the crumpled sheets, hiding his scar. "You're the only person…no one has said that to me since it happened."

I lean forward, tilting his chin with my hand so he's facing me directly. "I've never seen anyone as gorgeous as you." I run my lips across his cheek, coursing them over his scar. "Every time I'm near you my heart beats a little faster."

He takes a heavy swallow as his lips touch mine softly and gently. "I've never met anyone like you, Alexa. You're beautiful. Inside, outside, all of it."

I pull my body back up, rubbing my breasts along his chest as I do. "I wish I could stay in this room with you always."

"You can." He nods. "I never leave here."

"I know." I want to press him on that. I want him to come to my place so he can see my world the same way I see his. I want him to meet Kayla and Sadie. I want him to walk down the street holding my hand. I want our lives to exist beyond his apartment.

"What do you need to tell me?" His hand lazily runs across my right nipple. It instantly swells as an ache races through it.

"I told two people about us." I trace my fingers over his knuckles, silently encouraging him to twist my nipple again.

"Who?" His brows shoot up as his mouth curves into a subtle grin.

"Two of my friends." I close my eyes briefly. "Kayla and Sadie."

"Kayla and Sadie," he repeats back. "What did you tell Kayla and Sadie?"

"I told them that the Noah Foster was fucking me." I lean back and slowly pull my aching sex across his cock. The thick root presses against my clit, causing me to involuntarily moan.

He reaches to the edge of the bed where he threw several condom packages when I was undressing. "Did you tell them how good it was?" he growls before ripping one foil package open with his teeth.

I shift back giving him the access he needs to sheath his cock. He pulls quickly on my hips, directing me over him, grazing my folds across the hardness.

"Only Kayla," I murmur. "I told her."

"Goddamn you're so fucking wet." He glides my hips back until the tip of his cock is pressing against my entrance. "Tell me what you told, Kayla."

I groan as he pushes his thickness into me. It's so much. There's still a delicious pain whenever he enters me. His cock stretches my body. "That it was the best sex…" I moan loudly when he adjusts his hips and he hits my most sensitive spot. "The best sex I've ever had."

"I'm your best." He closes his eyes as his hands dart to my thighs. "You're my best."

I lean forward, my hands resting on either side of his head as I glide my hips over him, pulling his cock slowly deeper and then almost completely out. The sensation of the friction of the wide crown pulling against my moist tissues is sheer torture and heaven all rolled into one.

"I can't take it," he hisses between clenched teeth as he effortlessly rolls us over in one silky movement, our bodies still connected.

I groan at the sensation of his cock stretching me. I wrap my legs around his torso, giving him more depth of pleasure. I'm rewarded with a grunt as he finds his rhythm. Tonight it's slow, leisurely, graceful strokes.

"You're so perfect, Alexa." His hands grab mine and pull them over my head. "Your pussy is mine."

"Fuck me, Noah," I whisper into his mouth. "Take it. It's yours."

His eyes bore into mine as he thrusts deeper with each stroke. "You love when I fuck you."

"I love it," I parrot back, twisting my hips to meet his. I feel the edge of an orgasm tempting me already. My sex clenches around his cock, my body readying for its climax.

"Come beautiful Alexa," he growls against my lips. "Show me what I do to you."

I cry his name loudly as the tension breaks through me. My body trembles. I can't stop it. I won't. I let the orgasm wash over me as he thrusts even harder.

He pulls harder on my hands, stretching me further, driving his cock into me with a deep grunt with each surge of his hips. He pulls back as he calls my name before his teeth grab the flesh above my nipple and he pumps out his own heated desire.

Chapter 9

"You haven't told me much about your new job." His breath runs a path across my forehead as I lean on his chest.

I trace a finger along the intricate lines of the tattoo on his shoulder. "I love it," I whisper. I do love it. Teaching science to seven-year-olds was fast becoming my favorite part of each day. I knew that I'd enjoy teaching but now that I was getting to experience the hands-on time that I'd been craving, I have no question within my mind that I've made the right career choice.

"Do they call you Miss Jackson?" I can feel his lips curve into a wide smile against my forehead.

"Yes." I flatten my hand against the muscles of his abdomen. "I love working with them."

His chest lifts, then falls. "I used to take pictures of children. That was a lifetime ago."

My head darts up so I can look in his eyes. "You used to take pictures of children?"

"In college." He nods his chin. "At one of those department store photo departments."

"The ones with the gaudy cartoon backgrounds that children are terrified of?" I cross my arms across his chest as I watch his expression.

"Exactly like that."

"Was it fun?" I bite back a smile at the idea of Noah with children. He's so imposing and intimidating with his tattoos. He likely didn't have them back then. He didn't have the scar either.

He nods his head slowly up and down. "It was a blast."

"Maybe you can come visit my class one day." I brace for his anticipated reaction. "I can ask the principal. She might be okay with it." I doubt that she will. The moment I mention that I want to bring world renowned photographer Noah Foster to class she'll probably lock all the doors. A man who takes nude pictures for a living likely isn't welcome in her grade school. She's the definition of prim and proper. I still want him to know it's my wish.

His body tenses as he pulls back slightly. "I'll think about it."

"I'd love for you to see where I work," I add, pressing my luck. Pushing him to leave the apartment is treading on dangerous emotional ground. "If you don't want to come when the kids are there, maybe after school one day when the classroom is empty."

"Maybe." He brushes his lips over my forehead. "I'm going to get a beer. Do you want one?"

I shake my head as he slides his body from under mine. "No. I'm good." I'm far from good. Watching him retreat back into the sheltered cocoon he's built around himself is breaking my heart a little more each day.

***

"What do you want me to get you for your birthday?" Sadie clears the dinner plate from in front of me. "We could go somewhere for a weekend or maybe a spa day?"

"Sure, either of those would be great," I say with whatever genuine excitement I can muster. "It's still a couple of weeks away. We don't have to make plans yet, do we?"

"I talked to Kayla about your birthday dinner." She slides a bowl of gelato across the table towards me. "We're going to do it at Axel. You're good with that, right?"

I nod my head not certain that I heard everything she just said. "Whatever works for you is good."

"Is there anyone from the school you want to invite?"

I stare at her, watching her savor the taste of the cold treat. "From the school?"

"The people you work with there?" She cocks a sculpted brow. "Do you have friends there?"

I know she's talking about my birthday. I've heard the excitement ringing through her voice and we've each always taken on the task of planning the other's birthday celebration but the text that Brighton sent me right before I arrived at Sadie's place is haunting me.

We're not done. Call me. I'm in Boston.

The knowledge that Brighton is once again somewhere near me is jarring. Seeing him in Manhattan had unwound me completely and now that I'm spending more and more time with Noah, I just want Brighton to fade into my past as a horrible decision I once made.

"Alexa, where are you?" Sadie's standing next to me now, her hand resting on my shoulder. "What's wrong? Is it Noah?"

"No." I pat her hand with my own. "Noah and I are fine."

"Will he come to your birthday party?" She doesn't even try to mask the eagerness woven into the question. "I want to meet him so badly."

"I can ask him," I mutter under a half-breath. "I don't think he'll want to come though."

"You're dating now, aren't you?" She moves back around the table to sit across from me. "Or is it just one of those casual hook up things?"

"It's somewhere in the middle."

"What does that mean?" She scowls. "You're not letting him use you just for sex, are you?"

I laugh at the bold question. "If anyone is using anyone, it's me using him."

"He's that good, huh?" She bites her lip. "Better than anyone else?"

"He's in a class of his own." I wink across the table at her.

She stares at me, her eyes wide. "Do you see him a lot?"

"A few times a week," I offer. "I've been really busy with work and we're not moving too fast."

"That sounds like dating to me. You should ask him to come to your birthday party."

"I'll ask," I acquiesce. "Don't expect a miracle."

Chapter 10

"Have you sold any of the pictures from your show yet?" I sit with a sheet draped around my body, my back leaning against the headboard of Noah's bed.

"Why? Do you need a loan?" He pulls his head back a touch so he can look at me from his position at the foot of the bed. "You're not making enough on tips with your side job delivering sandwiches?"

"I never quite get the sandwich delivered, do I?" I cock my head to the side. I'd actually laughed out loud today when Noah texted me asking me to pick up a sandwich for him at the restaurant. He told me to put it on his tab there so I'd ordered twenty and spent the next ninety minutes near the homeless shelter a few blocks from his apartment visiting with the people who could use the food the most. "You ordered twenty sandwiches today, by the way."

"Twenty?" He lifts his head up so he can look directly at me. "I was starving."

"You were." I don't dive into an explanation. There's no need to.

"You're a generous soul, Alexa." His eyes narrow. "Have you always been?"

"No," I chuckle at the question. "I'm pretty self-centered. I'm like you."

A slow grin pours over his lips. "I'm self-centered?"

"Maybe that's not quite the right word." I pull my knees up, wrapping the sheet around them. The heat of the orgasm I had not more than a few minutes ago when Noah was inside of me, is now giving way to a chill. "You're arrogant, or maybe it's more about being in control."

"I like being in control." His hand brushes against his cheek and over the scar. "I've lost a lot in the moments when I haven't been in control."

"When you were stabbed?" Tempering the question isn't an option. My curiosity about what happened to Noah has never wavered. I haven't pressed the subject because it's always been obvious that talking about the scar is his least favorite thing to do.

All I know with certainty is that he loved a woman who loved another man and that man attacked Noah.

"I didn't see it coming." He rolls over so he can sit up on the bed. "I had no idea she was living with another man."

The words hit a place within me that instantly brings up Brighton's image. "How long were you two involved?"

"Months." He wrings his hands together, forming a firm ball and then letting them slide apart. "He was away all the time. I didn't ask her if she was involved with anyone. Why would I?"

I don't answer the rhetorical question. With Brighton it was different. I had researched him online after Sadie gave me his name. I had read all the articles from the papers in New York about how his girlfriend, Liz, was hurt in a serious car accident and how he had dropped everything to take her to Paris to get her the best care possible. I knew about her. I asked about her. In my sordid emotional threesome, Brighton was the liar.

"You said you loved her?" I whisper, wanting desperately to know about the woman he never speaks of.

"Very much," he offers. His face is impassive as he stares past me to a spot on the wall behind me. "She's the only woman I've ever loved."

"What's her name?" It's a detail that I've ached to know. The knowledge of it won't hold any particular meaning to me. That's not why I'm asking him. I want to see if he'll share. I want to know if that barrier that he's built around himself that day will start to fall.

"It's not important anymore." His words are clipped and terse. "It was a long time ago."

"How long?"

"A few years." He pushes his legs out as if he's about to stand but he doesn't. The way he's fisting his hands at his side is a clear indicator that he's restraining his desire to run from the room and hide from my questions.

"What happened to the man?" My throat tightens as the question leaves my lips. "The man who stabbed you...is he in jail?"

"He's dead." His dark eyes catch mine, his jaw tightens and he leans forward balancing his hand on the bed. "I killed him."

***

"You look terrified, Alexa." He's beside me now. "You're not scared of me, are you?"

The words aren't meant to taunt me. He's searching my face for a reaction and judging by the way his eyes keep darting to my legs, he's waiting for me to jump up and run for the hills. "I'm not." My voice is shaky, but the tone is even.

"You're lying." His finger catches my chin to pull my face towards his.

My eyes blaze down his cheek, marveling at the understated violence of the scar. The slight growth of beard does little to conceal it, the jagged edge jutting out from beneath it. The marred tissue so damaged that hair can't find its place there. It's become a part of his skin, a permanent fixture on his face. "You don't scare me." The words sound too defensive. If I'm being honest, he's imposing, dark and very intimidating.

"He was trying to kill her." His hand circles my chin, pulling it into his grasp. "He would have killed her if I hadn't done something. He stabbed me and when he thought I was done he turned around and stabbed her in the arm. He was going for her neck when I stopped him."

I open my lips to ask. I need to ask. I want to know how.

His eyes settle on my mouth. I watch in focused silence as he pulls his tongue across his own lips, moistening first the top and then the bottom. "I broke his neck." I pull back slightly but he stays me with his hand. He leans closer yet until his lips are hovering against mine. "I put my hands around his neck and I killed him."

I recoil sharply and his hand drops from my face, falling with a dull thud into his lap. He stares at it before he pulls his steely gaze back to me. The intensity is still there but it's shadowed by something else. Regret. It might be sadness. It's a veil of something that I haven't seen before.

I shift slightly, my hand involuntarily jumping to his cheek. I trace the scar with my finger, marvelling at the length of it. I stare at him in silence, the only sound in the room the rhythmic ticking of a clock on the wall behind us.

"I'll understand…" His breath stalls as his eyes lock with mine. "If you want to go."

"I'm not going anywhere."

Chapter 11

"It's my birthday next Friday." I slip my feet into the boots I left in Noah's living room before he pulled me into his bedroom. "There's going to be a party."

"With funny hats and streamers?" He smiles down at me. The darkness that had settled over his gaze when he was talking about the stabbing has now been replaced by a light behind his eyes. He's more open. I want to ask about the woman and what their relationship is like now but I can't. That window closed back in the bedroom when he pulled me into his arms and held me in silence.

"Sadie's planning it, so probably." I shrug with a small smile. "Do you want to come?"

His features soften. He shifts quickly from one foot to the other. "I don't know."

I reach up to run my finger along the frown line on his forehead. "It's okay if you don't want to." I wince after I say the words. "I mean, if you don't feel comfortable."

His shoulders slump forward a touch. "Where is at? Your place?"

"My place is as big as a closet." I roll my eyes. "It's at Axel. Sadie's husband owns it."

"Bernie will be there?" He crosses his arms across his chest before sliding his hand up to his face. "I like Bernie."

"Bernie isn't into me." I grab my chest. "It breaks my heart but I'm not his type."

"What's his type?" He taps his index finger against his lip. It does little to hide the grin that has spread across his face.

"You?" I tease. "He's seen you naked, hasn't he?" I nod down to where Noah's dick is hanging between his legs.

"More than once," he answers with effortless ease.

"Why don't you wear clothes?" I've asked him it before but I've never got a straight answer.

"I don't like clothes." He lifts his brows slightly. "You shouldn't wear clothes either."

"I agree," I admit. "I can't exactly work at the school naked though. There is a dress code."

"Their loss," he tosses back. "Let's talk about your birthday more."

I glance at my phone, realizing how late it's getting. I have to be at the school by seven in the morning. It's near two now so I only have a few hours to sleep. "Next time?" I touch his forearm. "I need to go. It's late."

"Tell me what you want for your birthday." He ignores my plea to leave.

"What I want?" I parrot back. "As in what I want for a gift?"

"Yes." A dazzling smile carries into his eyes. "If you could have anything in the world what would it be?"

I scratch my hairline as I study his expression. He's waiting impatiently for me to answer, shuffling back and forth on his heels. I soak in the sight of his relaxed stance, his beautiful body and his joy in asking me such a personal question.

I look down as I search for an answer. "There's one thing."

"Anything," he purrs. "Tell me what it is."

***

I stare in stunned silence, my mind trying to catch up to the images my eyes are absorbing. "Noah." His name escapes my lips in a heated rush. "I didn't mean this."

"You asked for a small print of one of your pictures." His broad arm sweeps across the bright room. I've noticed the closed door to this room each time I've been here but I've never asked what it contained. I'd just assumed it was another bedroom. "Choose one."

I reach for his arm to steady my balance. "I can't."

"Alexa." His grin is wide and genuine. "Choose one and I'll make a smaller print."

Setting off I start towards the first of more than a dozen large photographs hung on the walls of the room. Each a different image of me, all of them displaying my nude body but not one contains a hint of my face. I study one before moving to the next, marvelling in the detail, stunned by the beauty of my skin and the softness of the poses. The mole, I've always hated that sits above my right breast, looks perfect. The softness of my stomach that I often berate myself for only adds to the nuance of the poses. The sensuality each photograph exudes is subtle and understated. "These are so breathtaking, Noah."

"These are beautiful," he says, his breath rushing over my cheek as he leans down to kiss me softly. "The breathtaking ones are over here."

I turn abruptly and wrap my fingers in his hair, pulling his mouth into a lush, deep and heated kiss. "There are more?"

"Come." He sweeps my hand into his. "I'll show you."

I let him guide me to a large desk positioned near the doorway. Several computer monitors sit atop it, each displaying a different image.

"Look at this one." He points to the first monitor and it's a close up image of me in his bed. I'm smiling directly at the camera. My hair is a jumbled mess. My eyes are dancing with joy. "I took that after you woke up. I was telling you about how I became a photographer and you fell asleep."

I remember that moment. I look so peaceful in the picture. I look so completely different in it than when I look at myself in the mirror.

"This one is gorgeous." He pushes his hand towards another monitor on the opposite edge of the desk. "I stare at this one for hours."

I gaze at it and my breath stalls. I'm on my back, my hands lazily resting over my head, my lips slightly parted. "I look so different."

"No," he whispers into my neck. "You look exactly like that."

"That's not my favorite though." He touches a mouse sitting atop the desk and a monitor in the middle pops on. "This is the one I'll never get enough of."

I lower myself into the chair as my eyes lock on the photograph. My chin is tilted slightly to the left. I'm gazing into the distance and my bottom lip is caught between my top teeth. It's obvious from the angle of the image that I had no idea it was being taken. "When did you take this?"

"The first day." He falls to one knee next to the chair. "When I told you I was checking the lighting. I saw it that night when I was reviewing our work. That's when I knew you were the most beautiful thing I'd ever seen."

Chapter 12

"There's going to be a huge surprise at your birthday party."
Sadie lifts her head and offers an overly sweet smile.

"Is it a male stripper?" I bounce my eyebrows up and down
playfully. "Can you get him to dress up like a police officer? I have
this fantasy about being pulled over by a cop and frisked."

Her mouth literally falls open.

"That's not the surprise?" I throw my hands in the air.
"Dammit, Sadie. It's not that you baked cupcakes, is it?"

"You're teasing me." She breathes an overly dramatic sigh. "I
can't hire a male stripper. What would Hunter say?"

"Hunter is coming to my birthday party?" I hope that there's
no lingering tease in my tone. Sadie's husband has always been busy
when we've hung out. I'm not on his list of best friends and he sure
as hell isn't on mine. As much as I've tried to get over my initial
misgivings about him, I'll always remember how hard their budding
relationship was on my closest friend.

"He wants to be there," she says it a little too nonchalantly.

"That's because he thinks I'll trash the place if I get drunk."

"It's because of the huge surprise we got you."

I squeeze my eyes shut, trying to conjure up an image of
what the two of them could have gotten for me that is so
monumental that Hunter is going to forgo an evening with his son to
hang out with me. "Give me a hint." I open my eyes.

Her head shakes seamlessly back and forth. "No hints, Alexa.
It's three days away. You can wait."

I can wait. She's right about that. I don't even want to go to
the party knowing Noah likely won't show. I'd spoken to him on the
phone earlier today and with my rushed schedule this week because
of parent and teacher interviews in the evenings, we agreed that I'd
visit him at his apartment on Saturday for our own personal birthday
celebration. He hadn't mentioned my party and I knew that bringing
it up would only make Noah uncomfortable and would disappoint
me even more.

***

"It's a Brighton Beck original," Sadie screams as I pull on the edge of the patterned wrapping paper.

"God, no," I whisper under my breath. Please tell me that I misheard that. I rip the rest of the paper free and mutter a curse to myself. It's indeed a Brighton Beck original water color.

What. The. Fuck.

"Do you like it?" Sadie's arms are wrapped around my neck in what feels like a chokehold. The fact that I feel as though I can't breathe likely has very little to do with the fact that she's hugging me and more to do with the reminder of the man I wasted a semester in Paris on. I get it fate. This is what a cruel twist feels like.

"It's..." No. Just no. Please someone knock me unconscious and make this nightmare end. That is not Brighton walking through the doors of the restaurant. Where is the happy part of the birthday? So far, it's been shit. With a classroom of unruly children to manage on my own because Natalie had cramps, Noah's very brief text telling me to have a happy day and now Brighton's presence at my party, I may just give up birthdays all together for the remainder of my sad excuse for an existence.

"Is that Beck? Your Beck?" Kayla whispers into my ear. "Alexa? You were fucking Brighton Beck?"

"Don't remind me," I scowl. "Don't tell, Sadie. She worships the bastard."

Kayla gives me a weak hug from behind as Sadie races over to greet Brighton. His eyes drop briefly to her face before they settle back on me. My mind is telling me to grab my bag and run for the door, but I can't do that to Sadie. I need to swallow my pride, hide behind a mask of fake obliviousness and act like I actually don't know him.

"This is my friend, Alexa." Sadie holds out her hand to grab mine. "She's a big fan of yours."

Shut up, Sadie. Shut the hell up. I am not a fan of this man. I can't stand the sight of this man. "Hi," I manage in a weak voice.

"Happy Birthday, Alexa." He reaches to take my hand from Sadie's and pulls in to his mouth. His lips skirt over my palm before he gives it a tight squeeze. "You're lovely."

I can actually hear Sadie's heavy sigh at the words. She's never been quiet about her love for Brighton Beck and the fact that she has one of his paintings hanging in the bedroom of her apartment is reason enough for me to understand her deep fascination with him, but this, this is too much.

"You didn't have to come all the way to Boston for this," I say the words sweetly although their meaning contains a sharp bite. "I wish you wouldn't have come."

"Alexa," Sadie snaps. "Brighton took time out of his very busy schedule to come here for this. Don't be rude."

"I doubt that your friend is being intentionally rude, Sadie." Brighton flashes his signature dimpled grin. "She's just overwhelmed by my presence."

Seriously? Did he actually just say that I was overwhelmed by his presence? "It's not that," I intervene. "I just know that you have a girlfriend who needs your attention," I purr through clenched teeth. "It's everywhere in the papers. What is her name? Liz?"

"I heard about that." Sadie jumps in before Brighton can respond. "She was hurt very badly, wasn't she? We talked about it in class."

"In class?" His gaze narrows. "What do you mean?"

"Medical school," she says proudly. "We were talking about some of her injuries. The ones that the news was reporting on."

He nods briefly and his neck twitches. "I'd like a moment alone with your friend to explain the delicate subtleties of the painting you purchased for her."

"Of course." Sadie smiles as she falls for his bullshit, hook, line and sinker. "I'll be right over there if you need anything."

I lean back on my heel wanting to widen the distance between Brighton and I. "Why did you come? Why?"

"You've been ignoring me since I saw you in New York." He nods an acknowledgement to a couple standing several feet away from us. "We need to talk about things."

"There's nothing left to talk about." I dart my gaze back to where Sadie is standing next to Hunter. "My friend has no idea about what we did in Paris. She can't know."

He nods and looks past me. "You haven't let me explain a thing since you left Paris."

I pivot on my heel, wanting to turn and walk away but knowing if I do he'll chase me down. This is the moment in time that I've been dreading. It's when I have to face Brighton and finally put all the cards on the table. "Let's go outside." I point towards the door of the restaurant. "This is about to get ugly."

Chapter 13

Maybe it's supposed to be like this. Perhaps I was always meant to spend the night of my twenty-third birthday putting the past behind me. I've been avoiding discussing anything with Brighton to this point and now he's dropped from the universe into the middle of my birthday party. Tonight I am finally going to get the closure I so desperately need.

"I love you, Alexa."

Oh hell. No. Just no.

"I love you," he repeats as if I didn't hear it the first time.

"What?" I snap. "You didn't just say that to me."

"I did."

"Fuck you, Beck." My stomach tenses. "Don't pull that shit on me. You've never loved me. We both know it. You never said it."

"I'm saying it now."

My mouth hangs open for a second while I contemplate the words. "Why are you doing this?"

"I'm being honest," he goes on. "I was a coward in Paris. I'm not that man anymore."

"You're the same man." My tone is severe and clipped. "You haven't changed a bit."

He lowers his head and takes a heavy swallow. "She never loved me."

"Who?" I temper my pitch, not wanting to draw any more attention to us than is already there. Sadie keeps peering through the window to where the two of us are standing on the street in front of the restaurant. "Liz?"

He exhales harshly. "She's never gotten over the guy who died in the car that day. She can't get over him."

"What guy?" My response is intuitive, not introspective. I don't care what guy he's talking about. I don't care about any of it.

"She was with a man the night she got hurt," he says, his gaze darkening slightly. "He died in the car. She was in love with him."

"None of this matters to me." The words sound rushed and harsh. They are. I don't care who his girlfriend loves or who she used to love. I only care about my heart and Beck's the one who broke it.

"I fucked up in Paris." He shifts his lean body weight from one foot to another. "I brought her to that café so you'd see us."

"I know." I pull my hand across my face. "Why? Why would you do that to me?"

He doesn't look at me when he answers. "I was confused."

"Confused?" I bite out through clenched teeth. "Confused about what?"

"I was falling so hard and fast for you, Alexa." His voice is a tempered growl. "I thought Liz loved me and then when I was with you, I saw real love in your eyes. It scared the fuck out of me."

"Is everything okay?" Sadie's head juts out from around the doorway. "Brighton, is there anything you need?"

I close my eyes wishing that the last fifteen minutes of my life never happened.

***

"You can't leave yet." Sadie whines from behind the large wineglass that is at her lips. "It's early still. It's your birthday, Alexa."

I stare past her to where Brighton is seated. He's talking to a group of people I went to high school with. From the look of awe on each of their faces, they're smitten with his presence. I, on the other hand, have had more than my fill of Brighton Beck for the night. "It's been a long week with work and stuff," I lie convincingly. "I'm going to take off and crawl into bed."

"What about the painting?" She motions towards the gift that she and Hunter so graciously bought for me. Judging by the cost of Brighton's work, it must have cost several thousand dollars. I know they're not pinching any pennies, but the gesture is too much, especially since the artist in question just poured his heart out to me on the street.

"Can you take it home tonight and then I'll pick it up next week?"

I see disappointment wash over her face. I feel badly but there's no way I can have that painting in my apartment tonight. The emotional burden of its reminder is more than I can bear. I just want to go home, shut the world off and wish the past year of my life away.

"I'll bring it over on Monday night," she offers through a forced smile. "I'll bring Cory too. He likes hanging out at your place."

The suggestion that she bring her stepson is welcome. She typically only brings him with her when we're not seeing eye-to-eye on something. It's a subtle, yet telling, clue that she's not happy with me.

"I love you, Sadie." I pull her into a close embrace. "Thank you for everything. I loved my party."

She kisses my cheek softly before she pulls away. "This year is going to be amazing for you, Alexa. I can feel it."

I smile at her through heavy eyes. All I can feel is numbness and regret. Next year, I need to remind myself to insist on a party free birthday.

Chapter 14

I love Boston. I've always felt safe here. The ten block walk from Axel to my apartment is the perfect retreat from the suffocating evening I've had. I just need to soak in the cool night air, revel in the weekend crowds, and take a few deep breaths. Brighton's words are haunting me. I want to drop them at the side of the road and watch a bus trail over them, but they're in my brain, firmly encased.

I hear a loud roar behind me. I stop briefly to glance back. My eye latches on a crowd. The mix of men and women, my age, is a dull reminder of my college days. Now, that I'm getting out of bed and going to work each day, I feel more grown-up. The constant reminder that a lecture hall afforded me of my uncomplicated youth seems so foreign. My life has changed so much. I feel like one version of me boarded the plane bound for Paris and another stepped back onto American soil. I long for who I used to be, pre-Beck.

I watch as the crowd disperses after they've finished greeting another group that just arrived. One man, standing off in the distance, is misplaced. His clothing is thick and heavy for the warm night air. The baseball cap that is pulled over his brow conceals his face. He's dark, mysterious and as my father would say, "he's the reason you shouldn't walk alone at night."

I quicken my pace as I turn off the main street to begin the three block trek to the tiny walk up apartment I've been living in since I graduated from high school. The meager salary I had brought home when I worked at Star Bistro with Sadie wasn't enough to cover half of my rent, but the tips had given me the cushion I needed. I loved the independence being away from home gave me. More than that, I loved the solitude.

I sense a presence behind me and I turn quickly. The man with the ball cap is there, following my traveled path. I walk as fast as my heels will allow, longing for the security of my building. I fish in my bag for my cell phone, readying it in case I need to call for help.

I breathe a heavy sigh of relief as I see the dim light of my building just up the block. It's the only place in the world I feel safe anymore. The moment I returned from Paris, I went to my apartment, locking the door behind me for three full days before I reached out to anyone. I'd wept, grieved for the loss of Brighton's love and pulled all the strength I needed to face all my friends and family without a tear in sight.

I fumble with my key, pushing it into the heavy glass door. I scoot inside before it clicks to a locking position behind me. My eyes trail a path at the man in the ball cap as he crosses the street. I watch silently as a woman standing in front of a building there embraces him, pulling the cap off his head, revealing short white hair. They clasp hands tightly as they disappear into the distance. My unwarranted fear is more tied to Brighton's shocking presence than the man on the street. I have to calm my nerves down. I have to get a grip so I can deal with Brighton tomorrow. He's the real threat in my life. He's threatening to knock me emotionally off balance yet again and I can't let that happen.

I turn and face the dreaded three flights of stairs. I look down at my heels. "Hell, no." I laugh to myself as I slip them off and slowly pull my weary body up each step one at a time.

My phone rings as I near the top step. "Hello," I whisper into it, not wanting to wake any of my neighbors. *Neighbors* is a word that encompasses a friendly, helpful spirit. I should really call them frenemies. Any time I have my television or music playing beyond a hum, someone is pounding on my door telling me to "turn down the racket." This is my home though and after my encounter with Brighton, it's the only place I want to be.

"Alexa." My name is clipped as it flows through the line. "I've been trying to reach you all day."

"I'm sorry, mom." I sigh heavily. "I've been busy."

"I just called to wish you a happy birthday." There's no emotion in the words. She may as well be reading her grocery list to me.

"Sure," I snap back, the phone precariously balancing between my ear and my shoulder while I once again search for my keys. Why the hell did I dump them back in my bag after I opened the lobby door? "I need to go."

"Come over this weekend." It's a direct command, not a request. "I have a gift for you."

"I'll be there Sunday," I say into the phone. "Love you." It's an offering that is expected, not necessarily voluntarily. I love her. I do. It's just not words that have ever held a place within my family. We understand the sentiment is there, we don't often express it.

"Sunday, it is." There's a long, hesitant pause. "Me too."

I shake my head as I toss my phone back into my bag, my eyes desperately searching for my keys. I wish the super would have replaced at least one of the three burnt out light bulbs that illuminate this long narrow space. I wish I could clap my hands and my door would pop open.

"There you are…" my voice trails as I feel the cold metal in my palm just as a large, strong hand wraps itself firmly around my waist.

Chapter 15

"Don't scream." His deep voice growls into my ear. "Open the door."

I push back into him. I can't believe he's here. "Why are you here?"

"Open the door, Alexa." His lips curve into a smile against my neck. "I'm going to fuck you."

I almost moan from the promise. "Noah."

"If you don't open the door, I'll fuck you right here in the hallway."

I push the key into the lock with a shaking hand. He reaches around me to grab the doorknob. He twists it and we fly into the room together, the door swinging shut behind us.

He slides us both towards the wall, his massive frame guiding me with little resistance. I try desperately to spin around to look at him, but he's too big, too strong.

His hands roam across my dress looking for an opening. I scream when he rips the bodice apart, the fabric no match for his fists. He cups both my bare breasts and races his thumbs across my already swollen nipples. "I saw you," he hisses into my ear. "I saw the way your tits bounced when you danced."

My breath hitches at the confession. He saw me at Axel? He was there? I'd only danced briefly with Kayla in a corner when she played a song on her phone because we were both so bored. "You were there?"

His left hand falls to my thigh, his short nails tracing a path along the flesh. "You move your hips like you're slowly fucking when you dance."

I moan as his fingers skirt over the silk of my panties. "Noah, please."

"I kept thinking about how wet you were. How fucking wet you get." I groan as his hand dips into the back of my panties before he deftly pulls them into his fist and snaps them apart. "You're dripping wet right now. I know you are."

I whimper. I can't form any sort of coherent response. My body is literally aching for his. I reach back, clawing at his jeans, wanting to free his beautiful cock.

He twists me around swiftly, his hand around my waist before he falls to his knees on my floor. I have no time to react. His tongue is hot and focused along my folds. I wrap one hand into his hair, pulling his face closer, wanting to negate any distance that is between his mouth and my core.

"Fuck, your pussy is so good." His voice is a muffled hum. "I could do this forever and it would never be enough for me."

I arch my back against the wall and scream when he hoists my left leg over his shoulder.

"I'm going to fill you with my dick when you come." The promise reverberates through me, pulling me closer to the edge. "Come for me, beautiful Alexa. Do it."

I pull hard on his hair as I race to the edge of my desire. I feel the wetness seep from me and I'm rewarded with a moan as he laps greedily at me, purring my name into my flesh.

He finally stands and I see his face. His lips are moist in the light that is shadowing in from the window. His chin is damp and his hair a wickedly sexy mess. I hear the faint sound of a zipper being pulled. "Kiss me." His voice is gruff and intense.

I run my lips along his cheek before I graze them over his. The taste of his breath combined with my lust is fueling my desire even more. I sense his hands moving as I hear the sound of the condom wrapper tearing away.

"I'm going to fuck your beautiful pussy." He pushes my back against the wall, pulling both my legs up and around his waist. He slides into me harshly, abruptly and greedily.

My breasts are heavy and needy, my sex so wet and wanting. I cling tightly to him as he pounds his thick, swollen cock into my body over and over again, the entire time my name is falling from his lips with each deep thrust.

"You're so beautiful, Alexa." His lips trail over my cheek.

I scream as his teeth bear down on the tender flesh of my neck as he races to his own orgasm and pulls another from me.

***

I watch him sleep. After we'd fucked, he'd dragged me to my bed and he ate me with such fury that I came over and over again. Each orgasm was more intense and weakening then the last. Hours passed as he devoured my body. His hands reached every corner of my flesh; his words touched every fiber of my being. He'd finally fallen asleep when I begged him to allow me to get a drink of water. Now, an hour later, I can't bear to take my eyes off his beautiful face.

The quiet hum of a phone jars me and I jump to my feet. I need him to sleep if I'm going to have any chance to rest myself. He was so greedy and hungry for me. I want that again once we've both slept.

I scurry out into the main room to look for my purse so I can fetch my phone and turn it off. Before I can reach for it, I spot Noah's phone hanging out of his jeans pocket. Our clothes are a crumpled mess on the floor. Mine are torn and discarded hastily, his lay strewn in a pile together. I reach for the phone to silence it. My eyes course over the screen. It's a text message. Ari's name is on full display. We haven't spoken of the beautiful brunette who had tried to pry Noah's attention away from me at his gallery opening.

Call me Noah. It's about Camilla. She needs you.

I stare at the screen until it goes dark. Camilla. She's just another part of the riddle that is Noah Foster's complicated life.

Chapter 16

"I'm going downstairs to get some breakfast." I kick the edge of the bed to rouse him. He's been asleep for the past three hours. I couldn't find any peace after seeing that text message. I have no right to be as curious as I am about Ari and Camilla, but I can't help it. If either of them is Noah's version of Liz, I need to know now. I can't travel down that adulterous path again. I won't.

"You should come back to bed." He pulls a hand across his face and I can't help but notice how it stalls just as his fingers trace over the scar. "Alexa, come back to bed."

I've never been to bed, I want to say. Between our marathon fucking session, Brighton's sudden confession of love and Noah's mysterious text message it's a wonder I can string any coherent thoughts together. "I need some coffee."

"Hurry back." He sits up and swings his long legs over the side of my bed. I soak in the beauty of his tattoos and the stubble that had grazed my folds for hours last night when he was licking me.

"Come with me." They're wasted words. There's no way he's going to leap out of this bed, put on clothes and venture out into the light of day with me. I'm still in shuttered shock about the fact that he saw me at Axel and then followed me here.

Wait. He saw me at Axel. I was dancing with Kayla before Beck arrived. Noah must have seen me with Beck.

"Let me get dressed." He bounces to his feet, and grazes past me, his arm brushing against my shoulder. "I need to take a shower first."

I hear the washroom door shut behind him and the water pipes creak and groan as the first warm water of the day rushes through them. I sit on the edge of the bed, my foot tapping against the floor. How do I ask him about that message? What's the protocol for bringing something up that you discovered when you were looking at someone else's phone? What about Beck? Do I just casually throw in a comment about how he was part of my birthday celebration? So far, being twenty-three-years-old sucks balls.

"I think I'll hang out here while you grab a coffee." He appears, nude and wet at the bedroom door. "Do you have anything to eat here?"

"I can make you a sandwich when I get back," I say half-teasingly as I brush past him before grabbing my purse and sweater and heading out the door.

***

"There's a naked man in your apartment," Sadie is practically screaming the words into the phone. "Why is there a naked man here?"

"What?" I stop mid-step trying to juggle two cups of coffee in one hand, along with a bag of bagels. "Are you at my place?"

"I brought you the painting." It sounds like she's hyperventilating between words. "I came up and he was here."

"You saw him naked?"

"His bottom," she says in that charming, innocent way of hers. "Cory is with me. Get home now."

I wince when I hear that she brought her stepson along for the ride. Right now, there are two too many people in my apartment with Noah.

I race around the corner and hurriedly unlock the door of my building before I dart up the stairs. The door to my apartment is ajar so it takes little effort to push it open. I'm instantly greeted by the deep sound of Noah chuckling followed by Cory's raucous giggle.

"Take my picture." Cory is jumping up and down on the hardwood floor, his red hair bouncing with every movement.

"You need to stand still, champ." Noah aims his smartphone in Cory's direction. "You ready?"

"Ready," Cory says through a wide, very animated smile.

I stand in the doorway stunned by the sight in front of me. Sadie is leaning on the edge of the desk, soaking it all in with the same bewildered expression on her face as I have on mine.

Chapter 17

"Alexa, you're home." Cory races across the room to wrap his arms around my legs. "We waited forever for you."

"I was gone ten minutes, sweet stuff." I pat him on the top of his head. "I brought you a bagel."

"With cream cheese?" He reaches for the plain paper bag containing the breakfast I bought for Noah and I.

"You bet." I hand it carefully to him, trying desperately not to spill the hot coffee. "The other one is for my friend."

"For Noah?" Cory's dazzling smile melts my heart. "He's like Sadie."

"He likes Sadie," I repeat back. "Sadie is a sweetheart."

"No," Cory laughs with the abandon any four-year-old would have. "No, Daddy likes Sadie. Noah is like Sadie."

I hand one coffee to Noah before I kneel down and stare at Cory. "What do you mean?"

He holds the bag tightly in his hand as he walks to where Noah is seated on the couch. Thankfully his clothes now cover his body, the colorful tattoos on his arm still on display beneath the short sleeve of his t-shirt. Cory pats him on his knee and then reaches forward to grab Noah's shoulder with his small hand, pulling him towards him. "Noah has this." His fingers run carefully across Noah's cheek tracing along the scar. "Sadie has one here." His hand darts to his chest. "They're the same. They're special."

My eyes jump to Noah's face and within it I see a light that I've never seen before. He reaches down, carefully scoops Cory's tiny hand into his and kisses it softly.

***

"I'm sorry, Noah." I turn after closing my apartment door. "I had no idea they were coming."

He motions to the couch next to him. "Come, sit here."

I acquiesce and settle beside him. "I would have stayed. It must have been awkward when they rang the buzzer."

"That would have been less awkward than her using her spare key to unlock the door." He cocks a brow as he continues, "I'm pretty sure she saw my ass when I ran for the bedroom."

I purse my lips together. "No. She would have said something."

"She was blushing when I came back out." He finishes the last few drops of his coffee. "She brought you something."

I glance to the left to where the painting Sadie gave me last night is sitting on the floor. I don't know what to say. How do I bring up the fact that a painting done by my former lover is staring us both right in the face? "I don't want it."

"You don't want the painting?" A ghost of a smile skirts across his lips. "Did you tell her that?"

"No," I answer weakly. "It's too complicated. She idolizes Beck." I bite my tongue at the mention of his name.

"It's twisted that she'd give you something one of your past lovers created." The words hang heavy in the air between us. "Especially someone you cared so much for."

The reminder bites. He's skating around the issue. If he's not going to dive headfirst into what happened at my party, I'll gladly take the lead. "You saw me talking to him, didn't you?"

His head darts to the side and he glances past me to the painting. "I was across the street on a bench. I saw the whole thing."

The whole thing? What the fuck does that mean? "You saw me talking to Brighton?"

"I saw Brighton pleading with you. I saw the way he was looking at you. I saw it all."

"You saw me talking to Brighton?" I repeat. "That's all you saw."

"I saw his hand on the small of your back when you two walked back inside." His fist clenches on his knee. "I saw him staring at you when you left."

"You came to my party and you watched me with him instead of telling me you were there?" I say breathlessly, closing my eyes. "Why? Why didn't you come inside?"

"You know why, Alexa." He leans back on the couch, creating a divide between us. "You fucking know why."

"The scar," I whisper the words. "You sat and watched me celebrating my birthday with my friends because of the scar."

"I came there…" He reaches to cradle my hand in his. "I wanted to come inside. I got as far as the door and when I looked in the windows there were so many people. "

"You were going to come inside?" The confession is shocking. I hadn't even considered that as a remote possibility. I'd jumped to the conclusion that he had stalked me from afar. I assumed he'd hidden in the shadows until I left so he could follow me home.

He exhales audibly, his chest sinking with the movement. "I left my apartment hoping I could make it inside to your party. I wanted to surprise you." His hand pulls mine to his lips. "I'm sorry I couldn't do it."

"No." I crawl onto his lap, straddling his legs. "No, please." I run my lips softly across his. "Knowing that you wanted to be there is the best gift anyone has ever given me."

"What about that?" He tips his head to the left as his arms circle my waist. "What are you going to do with that?"

"There's a silent auction at the school next week." I smile as I cup his cheeks in my hands. "It's a fundraiser for new playground equipment. I'll donate it."

He cocks a brow as he works to hold in a deep chuckle. "You're going to donate a Brighton Beck original to your school's auction?"

I nod, tracing his bottom lip with the pad of my thumb. "Maybe they'll be able to build the new playground after that."

"They'll be building a new fucking school with the money that will bring in."

I throw my head back in careless laughter. This is how every Saturday morning of my life should be.

Chapter 18

"You didn't mention how bad the scarring was." Sadie tosses her head to the side as she pulls her car into a parking stall in front of my mother's house. "I had no idea."

"What scar?" I ask tightly.

"The scar on his face." The words feel misplaced coming from her. I'd challenged her about her scar for the better part of a decade. She'd hidden it beneath baggy sweatshirts and high necked tops until Hunter helped her see the beauty in it. Of all the people I know, Sadie should be the most compassionate and understanding about Noah's scar.

"It's not that bad." I throw the words back at her harshly. "I don't even notice it anymore."

A smile pulls on the corner of her mouth. "You don't?"

"No," I bite back. "It's hard for him, Sadie. You should understand that."

"Oh, I do." She nods briskly. "I know how hard it is, Alexa. I'm just saying you made it sound as though it was barely noticeable."

"It's not that noticeable." I feel a defensive wave rush over me. If this is what Noah deals with when he ventures beyond the walls of his apartment, it's no wonder he's become such a recluse.

"You like him a lot, don't you?" She tips her head to the side as she opens her car door. "I could see it when you were looking at him yesterday."

I pull my hand through my hair, straightening the strands. "My mother is waiting for us. Let's just go in and get it over with."

She nods softly. "He likes you too."

"What?" I toss the word back over my shoulder as I slide my foot out the door and onto the curb.

"Noah Foster likes you too."

"I know he does." I pull in a heavy sigh. "I can't say the same for my mother so let's get the torture over with."

She laughs heartily. "We'll stay an hour and then we're going to the spa."

"Deal."

***

"It's rude to stare, Alexa."

I exhale sharply, pulling my body away from his. "I wasn't staring. I was admiring. They're different." I'd been studying his scar since I arrived at his apartment hours ago. It's not as bad as Sadie makes it out to be. It's actually beautiful. It's become part of the landscape of his face.

"Tell me about high school, Alexa." He pulls the camera to his eye and the sound of the shutter breaks through the silence that follows his words.

"High school, Alexa?" I furrow my brow. "Who the fuck is that?"

He laughs behind the lens. "She's the girl you were in high school. Tell me about her."

"She wasn't very bright." I follow the path of the camera as he jumps to his feet and hovers above me. His chiseled nude body once again comfortably on display.

"Why?" His voice is thick and deep. "What did she do that wasn't very bright?"

"No." I turn to the side, tucking the sheet around my breasts to shield them from the lens. "Let's talk about you."

"Me?" He falls to his knees. "What about me?"

I pull my hands to my face. I'd been in agony for days. I thought the new week would ease my mind over seeing that text message on Noah's phone but the long hours at work haven't lessened my curiosity at all. It's Wednesday now and the image of Ari's text message is still burning a hole inside of me. I have to find out what it means.

"I wanted to ask you about a woman." I'll ease into this slowly.

"What woman?" His dark eyes dance across my face. "One of the women in the portraits at the gallery?"

"No." He just gave me a perfect segue for my question. "There was a woman at the gallery. Her name was Ari I think."

He rolls back on his heels and the camera drops from his grasp onto the bed. "Arianna."

"Yes, her." I push my ass back so I can settle myself against the headboard. "Who is she?"

"A pain in my ass." The words are razor sharp. "She was part of my show last year."

"She's just a model?"

"No." His gaze is hard. "We're friends."

The words surprise me. The only friend I've heard Noah speak of is Brighton and since the encounter at the gallery, I highly doubt that they're on speaking terms. "Friends?"

His jaw tightens. "Yes." The word is clipped and direct. "Why are you asking?"

This is the point where I should confess that I read the text message from Ari about Camilla. This is where honesty becomes the best policy. This is where I hide behind my insecurities because I don't want to fuck this up by sounding accusatory when he was only helping a friend.

"She was intense at the gallery." I pull on the edge of the sheet. The tactic affords me an escape from having to make eye contact with him. "She really wanted to talk to you."

He leans forward until his forehead is pressing against mine. "If you have something you want to ask, Alexa, spit it out."

My breath hitches. I pull my hand across my breasts, pushing the soft sheet into them, wanting a barrier between Noah and me. I part my lips; my intention is to ask about Camilla. I need to ask. I'll doubt our connection if I don't.

"She's my friend, Alexa." He kisses the tip of my nose softly. "She's nothing more to me. Nothing."

"I…" my voice trails into the distance as he pulls his large frame from the bed and disappears down the hallway.

Chapter 19

"I booked us a table to Axel for eleven tonight." I stand at the doorway of his office, fully dressed. "We need to leave soon."

"Why would you do that?" He doesn't turn to look at me, his eyes holding steady on one of the portraits of my body hanging on the wall.

"The restaurant will be empty." I tread softly across the floor until I'm standing next to him. "Sadie arranged it for me."

He glances down at me. "Maybe another night. I'm not hungry."

I sigh softly, disappointment skirting the edges of it. "I am so I think I may just go."

"I don't know how to do this anymore."

My stomach drops at the confession. "Do what?"

"This." His gaze is back on the photograph. "Take pictures of women."

I feel a sigh of relief race through me. "I thought…"

"Don't think that, Alexa." He reaches for my hand without looking at me. "I don't know how to breathe without you anymore. Don't ever think that."

The tenderness in the words doesn't match his body language. He's withdrawn, distant and holding back. The only reassurance he's offering is his fingers woven together with mine.

"What do you mean, Noah?" I squeeze his hand looking for something, anything that he can offer to me. "Why can't you take pictures?"

"That is perfection." He pulls both our hands up into the air, his index finger pointing at my pictures on the wall. "You're perfection. How do I go back to taking pictures after this?"

"I'm not perfect," I shoot back. "I'm far from perfect."

"You can't see what I see." His tone is insistent and determined. "When I came to your birthday party I looked at women walking by while I sat on that bench. None of them compared to you. Not one was like you."

I stare up at him, the light catching his scar and illuminating it. "You can't see what I see either."

His eyes dart down to my face, his gaze searching mine. "No one sees me the way you do." Something sparks within him and a small smile pulls over his lips. "We have a date. Let me get dressed."

***

"How did you get a driver to come pick us up so quickly?" I stare across the candle lit table at his handsome face. "He was there right after you called for him."

"He works for my father." He takes a sip from the glass of red wine he ordered once we were seated. He had hesitated only briefly when we walked through the front doors of Axel. The moment he saw how dimly lit the room was and that the restaurant was vacant, the tightness in his shoulders had washed away.

"I'd like to meet your father."

"You've met him." He taps his fingers against the table. I can tell he's not completely comfortable by the way his eyes dart around the empty space.

"I've met your father?" I pick up the wine glass but quickly place it back down. I have to work early tomorrow morning and going in with a hangover is definitely going to get me fired before first period is even over.

"He was at the gallery." He leans back in his chair and crosses his left leg over the right. He looks striking in a light colored sweater and dark pants.

"I don't think we met." I chew on the edge of a breadstick. "I'm so hungry."

"You met." He sips from the glass again. "He can't stop talking about how beautiful you are."

"He's just like you." I narrow my eyes at him. "I only met one man. His name was Ron."

"Ron Foster." He follows my lead and munches on a breadstick too. "We flew to New York together."

"I thought you might have flown." I look over his shoulder to where the waiter is checking his smartphone. "I didn't see you on the train."

"I had a ticket for the train." He picks up a fork from the table and twirls it between his fingers. "I had to adjust my schedule."

I trace my finger along my eyebrow. Noah's continual insistence on explaining away his need to not be seen in public is starting to wear me down. "You can just say that you felt uncomfortable. You know I understand."

He leans forward, his hand pushing the wine glass to the side. "It wasn't that."

"What was it?"

"My show this year was going to be all you." His mouth curves. "Then we fucked."

"You were actually going to show my pictures?" I feel heat course over my face. I remember the trepidation I was feeling at the gallery before the photographs were revealed. I was lost in such confusion when I believed that Amy's picture was mine. The knowledge that Noah had actually considered constructing a show entirely of my photographs is jarring.

"I was." His eyes dance as they meet mine. "Then I tasted you and I felt myself inside of you. I saw the moment when you came and I couldn't share that with anyone else."

"When did you decide not to show my pictures?"

"The afternoon of the opening." He shakes his head slightly. "I called my dad. We pulled the photographs I used together and got them up minutes before the gallery opened."

"I had no idea."

Chapter 20

"Your auction item brought in more than enough money to complete the playground, Alexa," Natalie, the teacher assigned to guide me through my time at the grade school, says. "We're actually going to use some of the funds that are leftover to help with the school lunch program."

I feel my stomach tense at the proclamation. I'm grateful that Beck's painting is going to help such worthy causes but my continual refusal to speak with him is quickly becoming near impossible. I'd jumped into a taxi this morning when I saw him headed down the street towards my apartment. I had been avoiding him purposefully since seeing him at my birthday party two weeks ago. The wish I made when I blew out my candles was that he'd disappear from the continent, obviously that wish wasn't going to come true anytime soon. "I'm glad it helped," I offer.

"You do realize it was a Brighton Beck original?" The assumption beneath the question is glaringly obvious. I have no interest in sharing my connection with Brighton with anyone I work with. They don't need to know. I'm just glad that I hadn't given Sadie any of their names when it came time to draw up the guest list for my party. If I had, I'd been dodging questions about Brighton left and right.

"I heard that, yes." I don't add anything more. Maybe she'll drop the subject and take up where she left off last week when she was gossiping about what one of the fifth grade teachers eats for lunch.

"Do you know him?" It's much more direct than I expected.

"That's an odd question." No, Alexa. That's an odd response. She's looking for a yes or no answer. You're only pointing the spotlight at your guilty face when you answer simple questions like that.

"He said he knew you." She leans closer. I can hear the shift to gossip tone in her voice. "I called him to see if he could meet with the buyer and he mentioned you."

Holy shit. Goddamn my life to hell.

"We met briefly in Paris." It's not a complete lie. We had only met briefly the first day we met in the park. The next day we were in bed in my flat.

"He'll be here tomorrow night for the reception for the donors." She turns to leave the staff room. "He asked specifically for you to be here. It starts at seven."

***

"No. I don't see why you need to mention it, Lex." Kayla shakes her head from side-to-side as she lies on my bed.

"No?" I sigh deeply. "You don't think it's a lie of omission?"

"Tell me everything you know about Noah Foster. Go."

"What?" I move quickly and the sudden shift in weight causes her to roll to the side.

"Go," she repeats as she sits up straight.

"He's twenty-nine, hot, a photographer, his father's name is Ron, he lives downtown and he was stabbed." I stop short, not wanting to share Noah's confession about the night he was injured.

"That's it?"

"I guess." I search my mind for any other telling details. I'm not sure she needs to know that he's fucked hookers, has a friend named Arianna and knows some chick named Camilla who needs his help.

"He knows way more about you," she points out. "He even knows about your last lover."

"That's true." She's right. He does know much more about my life than I know about his. I wish he would share more but I know that the skeletons in his closet haunt him in a much deeper and profound way.

"What are you two anyway?"

"As in?" I lead her into a more detailed response.

"As in do you just fuck or is there something more?"

"There's something more." I relax my back. "We're getting closer. There's a lot I don't understand though."

"Don't tell him about Beck." She shifts her body so she's facing me directly. "I'll go with you tomorrow. I'll keep Beck occupied and we'll be out of there before eight."

She makes it sound so easy. In the back of my mind, I know there's no way in hell I'll be escaping an evening with Brighton Beck unscathed.

***

"What are your plans after graduation, Alexa?" Brighton stands next to me. I'd dodged him to this point while he was preoccupied with the couple who purchased his painting from the auction. It's five minutes to eight and Kayla's prediction has just fallen to the wayside.

I throw Kayla a hurried glance across the room but her feet don't move from where she's standing. She's been pulled into a discussion with one of the donors about a potential job after she graduates with her business degree. I now wish I would have continued standing next to her, listening to them banter about projections and forecasts. "To teach." The words slide across my lips as much to appease Brighton as to stop the gossip mongers that seem to live in the hallways of the school. I can't let my co-workers see me break apart at the seams because I'm standing less than a foot away from the man who betrayed me.

"Here?" It's a follow up response that I should have anticipated. Part of me hoped that I'd find some opening in the circle of teachers and I'd be able to duck into the background and slither out to Kayla's car without another word. Brighton's not about to let that happen.

"As much as I love everyone here…"I manage a smile over my clenched teeth." I love it here but there won't be any open positions in the fall. I'll just apply to be a substitute."

"I heard that there's a waiting list for that," Natalie interjects. "You may need to move to another state to find something."

"Great." I sigh deeply. Now everyone in the vicinity knows that I've wasted the past four years of my life on a career that has absolutely no good prospects.

"I'm on the board of a grade school in Paris." Brighton's hand jumps to my forearm. "It's a bilingual school, Alexa. I can guarantee you a job there."

"Oh wow." The thrill in Natalie's voice is evident. "What I wouldn't give to get a job in Paris. Alexa, you're going, right?"

I slowly pull my arm away from Brighton's grip. "That's something I'll definitely need to think about," I offer to those gathered around us. Going to Paris to work might have been a dream come true when I was in the middle of my affair with Brighton. Now it's the last place in the world I want to be.

"Alexa, a moment?" Brighton's arm jumps to my hip and before I have a chance to recoil, he's pulling me away from the group.

"Not now, Beck," I beg in a muted tone. "Don't make a scene. I need this to work for me so I can get my degree."

"I was serious about the job, Alexa." He pulls me into a quiet corner away from the continual buzz of the room. "It would be perfect for you."

"Will you be in Paris?" It's a question I'm not actually searching for an answer to. I just want him to admit that he's manipulating my career so he can get me back into his life.

"I'll move there for you." The words hold an empty promise.

"You moved there for Liz," I push back, blatantly aware of how juvenile I sound. Why do I keep bringing up his girlfriend? Each and every time I do that I punctuate the fact that it stung like hell when I found out they were still together.

"Liz and I aren't seeing each other anymore." The words slide from his tongue with an effortless ease that does little to reassure me.

"I've heard that before." I gaze past him to where Kayla is still engrossed in discussion. "I don't care if you're dating her or not. Hell, I don't give a shit if you marry her, Brighton. Please, just leave me alone."

"Is it because of Noah?" The question is so unexpected that it takes me a moment to absorb each of the words.

"Noah?" I spit his name out. "You think I don't want to go to Paris because of Noah?" He can't really be that dense, can he? Does he not understand that my life and my career aren't dependent on where any man lives?

"You're falling for him. I saw it on your face at the gallery."

The words bite even though there's no logical reason for the pain. I don't care what Brighton thinks. My heart held on so desperately to the promise of what I thought we could have been that I couldn't see him for who he truly was. Once I saw his face again that night, I realized that everything I wanted my life with him to be, I left back in that tiny rented flat above the café in Paris.

"You don't know what you saw." I work to even my tone. I don't want to draw any attention to the two of us. "What I feel, or don't feel, for Noah is none of your business."

"You are my business, Alexa." He steps forward as both his hands jump to my forearms. "I love you. Why the hell can't you understand that?"

"You love me now because she dumped you," I say bravely. "If she still wanted you, you would be back there, taking care of her."

"That's not true." His denial is vehement, strong and abrasive. "I came here for you."

"You came here because I was your second choice." I pull back and his hands drop. "I will always be your second choice."

"You're his second choice too." He leans in as the words flow quickly from his lips. "When she takes him back, he'll drop you in a second."

I know I shouldn't give him the satisfaction of my curiosity. I know that I should pivot on my heel and march out of the gallery, but I can't. I need to hear her name. I need to know who Noah would choose over me. "Who?"

"Noah." He cocks a brow. "I was talking about Noah."

"No," I spit out harshly. "Who? Who would Noah choose over me?"

The look he shoots me is a thinly masked combination of satisfaction and triumph. "Camilla."

I take a step back, her name hitting me as hard as a slap across the face. "Camilla," I repeat her name.

"He killed for her, Alexa." His eyes lock with mine. "He'd do it again."

Chapter 21

"You know that I donated that painting to my school's fundraiser, right?"

"Sure. Did it sell? Are they adding a new wing named after you?" The brilliant smile that washes over his face is breathtaking.

"No." I grin back, resting my back against the leather chair he carried into this office for me from the living room. "It did sell though."

"That's great." He stares at one of the large monitors on his desk. "I'm trying to get back into shooting."

I nod at the confession. We haven't talked about his inability to work since that night when we stood here together before we had dinner at Axel. I was waiting for the other foot to drop. I knew that eventually he'd start calling women up again, asking them to come to his apartment so he could photograph them.

"Is it still a picture or play thing when you call a woman?" That's meant to sound casual. Unfortunately, for me, there's too much spite woven into the words.

"A what?" He turns his face to the side to stare at me. "What does that mean?"

Just spit it out, Alexa. "Are you going to start fucking call girls again?" I stop myself for a moment. "I mean, unless you've never stopped."

"You're not serious?" He scans my face quickly before he pulls his eyes back to the monitor and the emails that he's been shifting through while we talk.

"I'm serious, Noah."

His bare shoulders tense before he swivels his office chair to the side so he's facing me directly. "Why would I fuck a call girl?"

"It's part of the process." I pull air quotes around the words. "That and being naked all the time." I dip my chin towards his glorious cock that is resting between his thighs.

"I'm not fucking anyone but you." His gaze stays focused on my eyes. "I will not be fucking anyone but you."

"Oh." That single word can't convey everything I'm feeling.

"Now that we've settled that." He turns back so he's facing his monitor. "What about that painting you donated to the school?"

The timing couldn't be much worse but I'd promised myself I would bring up seeing Brighton when I got here. The fact that Noah has been working has kept me out of his bed for the night. Surprisingly, that's a plus considering I'd never find the courage to ask about Brighton's comment about Camilla if Noah's head was buried between my thighs.

"When I'm done with this, I'm going to lick your beautiful pussy."

No. Please no. Do not say that.

"I can't stay long." It's a weak excuse. I need to bring Brighton up now before my window of opportunity disappears, or before Noah drops to his knees and uses his skillful tongue to make me forget my own name. "I saw Brighton," I blurt the words out in such a heated rush that I'm not sure they are even distinguishable from one another.

"When?" If he's surprised, he's a master at hiding it.

"Last night." I know I should say more than that. I need to move this conversation along so we're at a point where Noah is telling me that Camilla means nothing to him.

"At your place?" Again, the calm and cool nature of the question is disquieting. Part of me wants him to feel as torn up inside about Brighton as I do about Camilla, who at this point is a vague name that has floated out into the ether. Noah knows Brighton, he knows my history with the man and the fact that I just confessed that I saw him, doesn't even faze him.

I sit for a moment, staring at the way his long, elegant fingers strum against the barren steel of his desk. "The school had a reception for all the people who donated money. One of the teachers invited Brighton."

"Did you speak to him?" He starts typing on his keyboard. It's a motion that is both effortless and thoughtless. The gesture is speaking to how insignificant he feels it was that I have seen Brighton.

"We talked." I watch his hands, noticing how they don't break pace. "We spoke about you and Camilla." I throw any caution that I might have been holding within straight into the firestorm of wind that surrounds this topic. Way to fucking pace yourself, Alexa.

His hands stop in mid-air and the right one quickly bunches into a tight fist. He holds it that way for what feels like endless moments. In real time it can't be more than thirty seconds. Finally, he turns to me with a narrow gaze. "You have questions then." He's not asking if I do, he's assuming.

"I do."

He twists his chair around in one quick movement until he's facing me directly. His hands bolt to the arms of my chair trapping me in place. I see the thick vein in his neck pulse with each beat of his heart. The sheer magnetism that is rolling from his frame is overwhelming. He's right there, close, commanding and tense. "Well then, Alexa." He leans closer until his breath skirts over my forehead. "Why don't you tell me exactly what Brighton said about her?"

"Not much." I push my back into the soft leather of the chair seeking a sense of asylum. I need to create space between the two of us. "He said that's the name of the woman that you…"

"Camilla is the woman I loved." There's not an ounce of hesitation within the words. They are direct, genuine and meant to be taken very literally. "What brought on that conversation?"

I scan the room behind his face. My need to break the intensity between us my sole motivating factor. "He offered me a job."

I feel his hand graze my chin before his fingers bite into it, pulling my gaze quickly back to his. "Brighton offered you a job? Doing what, Alexa?"

My name slips from between his lips and it adds an extra layer of intimacy to the conversation. He said it to quiet my racing heart. He's trying to establish a connection between us in the midst of this discussion about the two people who once mattered the most in our respective lives. "He's on the board of a grade school in Paris and they need a teacher."

"You're moving to Paris?" His brow shoots us as the edge of his mouth tenses. "When were you going to share that with me?"

"I'm not moving." I break his gaze and my eyes fall to his chest. I focus on one line of his tattoos. It's so straight and unwavering. There's complete definition in it. All of the art that covers his body is like that. It flows flawlessly together, each design complimenting the next. It surrounds his body like a painting that has been stripped of its canvas and painted onto his flesh.

The way his shoulders surge forward at the words is unmistakable. His fingers relax on my chin but he maintains constant contact. "Tell me about Camilla. What did he say about her?"

I expect more of a reaction and I'm relieved that he says her name so naturally. His expression doesn't change as he asks the question. "He just said that she was the woman you were with when you were stabbed."

He loved her. It's a fact that we both know yet my mind won't allow the words to flow off my tongue. "He just announced that to you?"

"It came up in conversation." It's a small offering. Delving into the details of how Brighton and I got to the point where we were discussing Camilla seems unimportant right now. I just want to watch Noah's face, read between the handsome lines that are there to see which parts of him she still owns now, today, when he's just announced that I'm his only lover.

"You have questions about her." He's not asking if I do, he's opening the door for me to ask them.

"Just one." I jerk my chin away. I can't feel his touch when I ask this. I don't want the sensation of our bodies being connected in any way to mar his response. I want him open, direct and unyielding in his honesty when I ask about the text message I saw.

"I don't love her anymore, Alexa." His biceps flex as he pulls the heavy leather chair closer to him. "I don't want to love her. I want to be with you."

I set my hands over his, marvelling in how much larger his are. I lean forward and rest my forehead against his. "No more questions, Noah."

A ghost of a very thin smile skirts across his mouth. "I'm taking you to my bed. You're never leaving."

Chapter 22

"Kayla told me that Brighton offered you a job in Paris." Her tone is even and unemotional. Seeing how she can't disguise how excited she is when there's a sale on apples at the market, I'm assuming she's not thrilled with the idea.

"I'm not going." I take a small sip of the iced tea she got for me when I arrived at Axel.

"Why would he offer you a job?"

It's a very logical question. A world famous water color artist breezes into town, creates a stunning masterpiece to sell her to gift to me for my birthday and then offers me a job at a school that he's on the board of. "Why does Brighton Beck do anything? He's an artist, Sadie. They're eccentric."

"Is Noah like that?" She sips from her own glass.

"Noah isn't like Brighton at all." The only thing the two men have in common is that they're gifted at creating art that many people find a need to pay exorbitant amounts of money for.

She looks down at a stack of papers she's pulled from her bag. "How are things with you two?"

I hesitate briefly while I stop to distinguish whether she's asking about how things are between Brighton and I or Noah and I. She's still blissfully unaware that I had an affair with Brighton in Paris. I need to confess that sin to her one day. I have to. We've always shared everything and so far since I've returned from my semester abroad, I've been juggling more secrets than I can manage. Telling her about Brighton and about how Noah got his scar is inevitable. I just need to find the right moment to broach it all so that she has time to absorb it. "Noah and I are good. I haven't seen him a lot this week because I've been busy with work."

"He's supportive of that?" Her mouth twitches with the question.

"Very." I smile back at her. I love how protective she's become of my career choice. When I first told her I was chasing a degree in education, she accused me of only being in it for the benefit of the extra-long winter and summer vacations. Once she understood that my love of children as the foundation for my need to teach, she'd become my biggest advocate, helping me choose my classes and being my study partner even when her own course load was weighing her down.

"I like that." She leaves through the papers on the table. "These are some of my study notes."

"Study notes?" I laugh as I see all the hurried handwriting. "Why don't you take your tablet to class?"

"I keep forgetting it." She taps herself on the forehead. "My mind is so foggy lately."

"Is everything okay?" I ask. Sadie's always been the most organized person I know. She's had her entire life planned out since we were in middle school.

"It's fine." She pulls one sheet out with a wide grin. "This is what I was looking for. I need to study so…"

"So scram?" I tease. "You want me to get lost?"

She nods playfully. "It's a big exam. I need to study."

"Consider me gone." I stand and reach over to kiss her on the cheek before heading out the front door of the restaurant into the crowded early evening pedestrian traffic.

***

"Christ, Alexa." He moans into my shoulder. "How do you take me so deep?"

I push back with my ass into his groin, pulling the wide crest of the tip of his cock over my folds before I pull him within again. "My body was made for yours," I whisper into the sheets on his bed.

"I've never fucked anyone like you." His hands grip tightly to my hips, pulling them up from the bed. "I could pound my cock into you like this for hours."

"Promise it," I whimper as he pushes even harder. "Promise you'll fuck me for hours."

He rears back and plunges his cock to its depth. My name flows from his lips in a heated rush.

I scream out sharply from the bite of exquisite pain but my body needs more. I slide to my knees, pushing my ass back towards him, putting it on full display. "Fuck me as hard as you can, Noah. Do it."

"As hard as I can?" He pulls himself from my channel and guides the tip of his cock over my clit. "You want me to pound your pussy." He pushes inside violently until he's balls deep and my body reacts. I jump forward a touch but his hands hold steady to my hips pulling me back, impaling me on his thick root.

"Ah, fuck." The words flows across my lips without any thought of purpose. I can't control myself when it's like this. I can't stop the sheer need of my flesh for contact with his. It aches for it. I crave it just like I crave air.

"Goddamn you." He thrusts himself into me over and over again. The sheer force of every drive pulls the bed along the hardwood floors. He grabs my hair and yanks hard on it, my neck snapping back.

"Harder, Noah," I plead. "Fuck me harder."

He acquiesces and digs his fingers into my hip, pushing with everything he has." Feel my dick, Alexa. Feel it inside that wet pussy."

I love the way he talks to me when he's fucking me. "Harder," I urge.

A deep grunt escapes his lips as both hands grab tightly to my hips and drive my body back onto his. "You're going to come for me, Alexa. I feel it around my cock."

The words toss me over the edge and I blindly grab for anything to center my release. My hands bunch into the mangled bed sheets, pulling them between my fingers as my sweat soaked forehead pushes into the mattress, the fabric of the linens stifling my screams.

"Milk me," he growls behind me. "Milk my dick with your body."

I rise to the challenge and glide my hips forward and back, sliding his cock within my body. I push myself back harshly as he ups the tempo again, driving his wide, swollen flesh into me until a litany of curse words fall from his lips as he pumps his desire from his body.

Chapter 23

"Tomorrow night we're going on a date." He tenderly reaches down to pull the zipper of my sweater up so it's closed.

"A real date?" I eye him suspiciously. "Like a date where you have to wear clothes?"

His eyes drop to his naked groin. "I thought you liked me without clothes." The words are playful.

"I do," I say before pulling my messy hair into a tight ponytail. "Where are we going on our date?"

"You'll see." The spark in his eyes is irresistible.

"Are you going to pick me up?" I trace a path down his chest with my hand soaking in the definition of his abdomen.

"I'll text you the address and you can meet me there at nine." His brow shoots up with expectation. "Is that okay?"

It wasn't everything I wanted but in Noah Foster's world it was a huge step. "It's perfect, Noah."

"Tomorrow it is." His lips slide softly over mine. "I'll miss your beautiful face until then."

***

"You're Alexa, aren't you?" A woman's voice calls to me just as I feel a tap on my shoulder.

I turn abruptly, jarred from my thoughts of Noah's promise of our date tomorrow evening. I've just stepped onto the quiet sidewalk from his apartment when she's there, saying my name with an understated elegance that is unmistakable. "It's Ari, right?"

"It is." She nods as she pulls on the collar of her coat. "I take it you were just with Noah?"

The question speaks of a natural familiarity that we don't possess. "Are you here to see him?" The tone of my voice even surprises me.

"Yes." She glances down at her phone, the movement causing the curled locks of her long brown hair to bounce against her shoulders. "He texted me that he's free now and I can go up."

I taste the bitter bite of jealousy course through me. The fact that Noah reached for his phone within moments after I left his apartment is only shadowed by the knowledge that she was lurking nearby waiting to pounce. "Enjoy your visit." Small talk with Ari isn't going to appease any of my lingering doubts about Noah's connection to her or Camilla.

"He's using you." There's no hiding behind the words. She's saying them with a brazen boldness that is both unsettling and impressive. We don't know one another. We've exchanged vacant pleasantries twice and she feels confident enough to spit out something as vile as that.

"You don't know anything about my relationship with Noah," I push back. "Nothing."

"Really, Alexa?" She taps her expensive heel on the pavement. "I know that you used to fuck his friend."

I recoil from the confession. Noah told her about Brighton and I? Why would he do that? "Noah told you that?" It's an empty question. There's no possible way she'd know about Brighton and I unless the information had come from Noah himself.

"Noah tells me everything." A chuckle chases the words. "He's my best friend."

His words about her being a friend haunt me. He said she meant nothing beyond that, yet he's confiding personal details of my life in her. "Lucky you," I spit back.

"You're just his current fuck." The words are harsh and misplaced coming from her. At first glance, she's the epitome of grace and culture. I feel completely mismatched as I stand on the sidewalk admiring her expensive clothes and her perfectly styled hair and makeup.

"He hasn't fucked you, has he?"

Her eyes narrow as she studies my face. "He wouldn't fuck me."

There's a challenge beneath the words. "Why?" I can't resist. I need to know why.

"He loves me." She tips forward on one heel. "I'm not like you. I'll be here long after he's done with you. You're filling time until she comes back."

The words tear through me. She's talking about Camilla. I know she is. Whatever the fuck was going on with Ari and Noah didn't matter anymore. It was Camilla I needed to worry about. There were too many whispered threats about her for it to mean nothing at all.

Chapter 24

"Did you have fun at the movie?" Noah scoops my hand into his as he opens the door of his apartment. Sitting in the back of the almost barren movie theatre, while we held hands and ate popcorn should have fueled me completely. It was what I had been wanting for weeks. Getting Noah to venture outside the walls of his apartment was everything I wished for, until Ari had stopped me on the street the other night. Now, all I longed for was the truth about what Camilla really meant to him.

"I had a lot of fun."

"We can do it again if you want." He pulls the sweater he's wearing over his head before he unbuttons his jeans letting them fall to the floor.

"Were you nude when Ari came over last night?"

His back is to me now and I watch as his shoulders tense with the question. "How did you know Ari was here?"

"I ran into her outside the building." I kick off my heels and slide the sweater I'm wearing off my shoulders. "She was on her way up."

"She didn't mention seeing you." He turns and his eyes dart past me to the windows that overlook Boston's breathtaking skyline.

"Did you put on pants before you saw her?"

"She's seen me naked, Alexa." He exhales audibly. "It's not a big deal."

It's not a big deal? "When did she see you naked?"

"I shot her for my show last year." His face is calm and expressionless. "You know my process."

"You've seen her naked too," I whisper. Why hadn't I realized that fact until now? He's seen so many beautiful women in all their nude glory.

"It's just skin." He brushes past me and I feel more exposed than he is, even though I'm completely dressed.

"We need to talk about something, Noah."

"Do you want a beer?" He disappears around the corner. I can head his padded footsteps traveling down the hallway to the kitchen.

"I don't want anything," I call after him. I just want to know about Camilla.

"Sit down, Alexa." He rounds the corner, a tall bottle of beer dangling from his fingertips. "Is it about Ari?"

I watch as he sits on the couch, his long legs crossing. He absentmindedly touches the tip of his penis, tucking it between the valley that has formed between the convex contour of his legs.

"You're so comfortable without clothes." It's not a surprised proclamation. It's a simple statement.

"I like being nude." He raises the bottle in the air before he takes a heavy swallow. "I love seeing beautiful women nude. Seeing Ari nude didn't mean anything."

He's trying to reassure me but I suddenly feel as though I'm suffocating beneath the knowledge of how many women have soaked in the beauty of his sculpted, tattooed frame. How many women have looked at his beautiful cock and wanted to taste it? How many have actually felt him inside of them? How did I not consider any of this before this moment?

"What about Camilla?"

"Camilla?" His back leaves the couch as his entire body tenses in one swift movement. He brings the bottle back to his lips, almost emptying the contents in a single gulp. I watch the muscles of his neck as he gracefully swallows.

"Noah." I move to sit on the edge of the coffee table so my knees are touching his. "Tell me about her. Tell me about what she means to you."

He shakes his head from side-to-side before draining the bottle dry. "I told you, Alexa. Camilla and I are over."

"People keep saying that's not true." I scratch my upper lip. "Ari said that you were using me until Camilla comes back. I don't know that that means but I did that with Liz. Brighton's Liz…" I stammer before I catch my breath. "I can't do it again. I won't get more invested in this if there's a chance you're getting back together with her."

He places the bottle down next to my thigh as he leans forward. "I told you that Camilla is in my past. I don't give a fuck what Ari or Brighton or anyone else said to you about her. Ari and Camilla are old friends. She's protective of her. It's nothing." He reaches for my hands, pulling them into his. "I am telling you that she and I are over. I haven't seen her in months. I don't want to see her. I sure as hell don't want to be with her."

The words are slow, direct and filled with quiet emotion. His eyes never waver from my face. His hands cradle mine tightly.

"I want to be with you, Alexa." He swallows hard. "You are my future. She is in my past. Don't listen to anyone who tells you differently."

"Who ended it, Noah?"

He cocks a brow. The question has surprised him. "It doesn't matter, Alexa."

I know from my experience with Brighton that it does matter. Liz dumped him and that's why he wanted me. It's my insecurities begging for an answer to the question, but I need it. I need him to tell me. "It matters to me."

"She ended it." He hands his head down. "I thought we'd be together after the attack, but she ended it. She said my scars remind her too much of him."

"Have you tried to get her back since?" Apparently self-torture is on my menu for tonight. I may as well drive a knife through my own heart. Why am I pushing this? Why can't I just leave this alone?

"For a long time all I wanted was her." He closes the distance between us, shifting his body so he's hovering on the edge of the couch.

I nod. I knew it. Brighton and Ari may have had their own motivations for saying what they did, but the alignment of their words wasn't coincidental. They've seen parts of Noah I never have. "Does part of you still want her?"

"I might have until you walked into my apartment." Reaching down he catches my thighs in his grasp and pulls me onto his lap. "No one on this earth is as important to me as you. No one, Alexa."

I push my face into his neck, feel him wrap his arms around me as I close my eyes and give in to the promise of his words.

Chapter 25

"Brighton keeps pushing me about working at that school in Paris." I flash the screen of my smartphone in Kayla's direction. "This is the third text this week he's sent me about it."

She shakes her head before she speaks. "Do you think you'd take it if Noah wasn't in the picture?"

It's a question I've never even considered. I'd like to think my decision to cut all ties with Brighton is about my own internal strength. Maybe it does have more to do with what I'm feeling for Noah than I've been admitting. "I haven't thought about it," I confess.

"You're not going to wake up months from now and regret that you didn't go to France, are you?" She cocks a brow as she picks at the bowl of pasta we prepared together in my small kitchen.

"No." I laugh. "Going to Paris means being with Brighton. I can't do that. Even if Noah dumped me, I wouldn't do that." The mere suggestion of my relationship with Noah ending bites into me.

"I'd say that you are officially over Brighton Beck now." She twirls her fork in the air in a mock sign of declaration. "That means I'm free and clear to jump his bones."

I wince at the announcement. "Have had it if you want." I tip my own fork in her direction. "Don't say I didn't warn you. Those artsy types are crazy as hell."

***

"I want us to go away for the weekend." Noah runs his hands over my bare back, pulling my body into his. We've just spent the past hour in his bed, his tongue, teeth and lips coaxing one intense orgasm after another from me. He insisted I not mount his beautiful cock until he held me.

"Where?" I'm almost giddy with the promise of a weekend away with him. After all the Brighton and Ari bullshit, we need time to shelter together into our own cocoon. Doing that in another city is exciting and it means that Noah is finally feeling comfortable enough to venture into the world with me.

"I thought we could go back to New York." His lips rest against my forehead. "I want to show you my favorite places there. Places I loved going to before the attack."

"I'd love that." I pull my hand across his broad chest. "A weekend in New York with you would be magical to me."

"Magical?" I can feel his smile on my skin. "I love how you love life, Alexa. I need that."

"I'll show you how to love every moment." I close my eyes, soaking in how perfect it feels to be this close to him. "We'll love them together."

"I guess I'll need to pack for this. I can't walk around Manhattan with my dick hanging out, can I?"

I shove at his hips but he's so heavy and strong. "You're hilarious."

"Come over on Friday afternoon when you're done class and you can help me pack. Bring your suitcase," he says softly. "We'll stay until Sunday night."

"I'll be here." I slide down his body, pulling the sheet aside revealing his erection. "I need to do this first," I whisper as I pull the thick crown between my lips.

"Yes," he hisses as his fingers weave through my hair. "Suck it hard, Alexa. Suck it good."

Chapter 26

"I'm leaving for Paris tomorrow." He's standing in my doorway. I wasn't supposed to see him again. My heart didn't want that. I wanted him to fuck off and leave me alone.

"I don't care, Beck." I reach to pick up my overnight bag and grab my keys from the coffee table. "I'm on my way out."

"You're leaving?" His blue eyes take everything in. "Where are you going?"

"I'm going on a weekend trip." I push past him and shut my apartment door with a thud. I push the key in, hinging the lock. "I need to go now."

"With Noah?" he asks gruffly. "Have you talked to him today?"

"That's none of your business." The question jars me more than he realizes. I had tried to call Noah twice to confirm the time he had booked for our train ride to Manhattan. Both times the calls had gone to voicemail.

"I saw him earlier," he admits. "We talked about you."

I know that I should ask for all the details but Brighton will slant them in his direction so I'll question the very fabric of my connection with Noah. I'm not about to let him, or anyone, steal this weekend away from us. It means too much to me. It's the start of a new beginning for Noah and me. It's the start of a life outside the emotional prison he's been keeping himself in.

"I'm late, Brighton." I start the steep descent of the stairs down to the lobby of my building.

"Alexa." He catches my elbow and I wobble precariously on the top step. I fear, for just a brief moment, that I'll fall. I instinctively reach out to grab his hand.

"Brighton, I need to go." I stare into his eyes. Anything that may have been there the night I saw him at the gallery in New York is now gone. All I see now, when I look at him, is a moment in Paris.

He nods and it's as if he finally sees it too. "I'm a phone call away. If you ever need me, I'll be on the first flight back here."

It's a tender promise that I know I'll never take him up on. When I walk out of the door and get into a taxi to take me to Noah's apartment, Brighton will officially become a thread of the fabric of my past. I can finally put that part of my life to rest, right where it belongs.

***

I glance down that the plain brown bag from Axel. Picking up a sandwich for our train ride is meant to pull at Noah's heartstrings. I know he considers it a special part of our connection, so surprising him with it seems like the ideal way to start our weekend of new beginnings. I'm excited to tell him that Brighton is leaving. He probably already knows. Brighton likely wanted to talk to Noah about his plans. I'm hopeful that he hasn't completely spoiled Noah's mood for me. Leave it to Brighton to try to fuck up my life even when he's heading out of it for good.

I wait until the doorman whizzes back down in the elevator before I knock at the door. I don't hear footsteps but I know that Noah is in there, waiting for me to help him pack the few items of clothing that he does own. I knock again, much harder this time. I'm almost bouncing up and down from the sheer excitement of what's awaiting both of us in New York.

The door opens slowly and I instantly know that it's not Noah holding onto the other side of the door handle. I spot her feet first. Her toenails are painted a subtle shade of pink. My eyes trail up her bare legs to the bottom of a white bed sheet that is wrapped around her petite frame. My breath hitches as my gaze stops on her face. I stare at her in wonder. My voice is caught somewhere inside of me.

"Can I help you?"

"Noah," I manage to spit out in haste. "I'm here to see him."

Her eyes drop to the bag in my hand. I left my suitcase in the lobby, knowing that within minutes Noah and I would be back down on our way to the train station.

"Are you delivering something?" Her eyes meet mine again and I see a reflection of my own question there. She's staring at me with the same wonder in her expression.

"Is he here?" Just as the question leaves my lips I hear his voice in the background. I can't make out the words. Maybe I don't want to make them out.

"You look like me," she whispers as she reaches to take the bag from my grasp. My eyes settle on her forearm and the jagged scar that adorns it. "You look almost exactly like me."

I stare at the scar before pulling my eyes past her face to where Noah is now standing in the apartment, his nude, wet body just feet behind her. He's drying his hair with a towel.

"Noah, look how much the delivery girl looks like me." There's a carefree lilt in her voice. "We could be twins."

She's right. We could be twins. She looks so much like me. More than Amy did. More than any of the blonde, blue-eyed women in the portraits did. More than any woman he's photographed, or called an agency for, or fucked has. This woman bears a striking resemblance to me and suddenly it all makes sense.

"What are the chances my random twin would be delivering your food?" She darts her head back to look at him.

It's not random. That's why I'm perfection to him. I'm her. I'm Camilla without the scar.

I take a step forward.

I need to talk to him.

I need to understand what's happening.

"Camilla." Her name is a growl that comes from deep within him. "Give us a minute."

"You can tip her in front of me." She doesn't move. "Get rid of her, Noah. We have a lot to talk about."

"Go in the other room." His hand sweeps down the hallway and she walks away, her bare feet moving quickly along the floor.

"Noah," I say in a tone that I can't even hear. "What is going on?"

He doesn't respond. He stares blankly at my face, his eyes studying each of my features intently.

"What is going on?" I repeat louder and more clearly.

"You need to go, Alexa."

I reach for his arm but he pulls back. I stumble forward before I regain my footing. "No. I'm not going anywhere."

"Please, Alexa. Just go."

The door opens under his heavy hand. His eyes don't meet mine as I walk back into the hallway. The dull thud of the door slamming shut the only sound in the empty space.

VAIN

PART THREE

Chapter 1

No. This is not how this goes. I'm not going to get on that elevator and ride away into the sunset in despair while he drives his dick into my doppelganger's vagina. No. That is not happening. This is too reminiscent of Paris. Did Brighton come over here and give Noah a primer on how to break my heart? Did he tell Noah to have Camilla on stand-by so when I showed up, he could make it clear that she was the one for him and I was nothing? I'm not doing this again. This is beyond fucked up. I've stood here just outside his door, in utter silence, for the past ten minutes, my mind replaying over and over again what must be going on inside the apartment.

I twist back around and slam my fist against the heavy wooden door. I take in a deep breath, wanting to calm my heart. It's not only racing, it's braking hard and fast, skipping beats in the process.

"I told you to go." He's dressed now in jeans that hang low on his hips. The trail of dark hair that runs across his broad, tattooed chest forges a path down his toned abs before it dips below the waistband.

"What the hell is going on, Noah?" I ask, wishing my voice didn't sound so high pitched. I know he can hear every emotion that is coursing throughout my body in my tone. I have to stay calm. I have to get some understanding so I don't spend the next six months of my life trying to piece together what happened. I went down that road with Brighton, there's no goddamn way I'm doing it again.

He rubs his hand across his forehead. "This is a really bad time, Alexa. You need to leave."

"I'm not going anywhere." I dart my eyes past his shoulder to the empty living room. I strain to hear Camilla's voice but there's nothing but stillness in the space. "I want to come in."

He brushes against me before stabbing his finger into the elevator call button. "Go now."

"No." I don't waste a movement as I skirt over the threshold and into his apartment.

His strong hand is on my elbow in an instant. "You can't be here," he murmurs. "I'm busy right now."

"Doing what?" The subtle suggestion of him being busy with Camilla bites into me. I'll never shake the image of her wrapped in that bed sheet from my mind. "Why is she here? You should have told me she looks just like me."

"Camilla?" His jaw firms. "She doesn't look just like you. There's a slight resemblance."

I study his expression for any sign of humor. He's not joking. He's seriously just said that. "I look identical to her."

His lips purse together and his eyes run slowly over my face. "She's ordinary, Alexa. You're beautiful. "

"That's such bullshit," I spit the words out in a heated rush. "You picked me because I look exactly like her."

"I was attracted to you at first because you reminded me of her," he admits. "Then you opened your mouth and I realized you're the exact opposite of her."

"What does that mean?"

"You're kind. You're honest. You're strong." A small smile slides across his mouth. "I've never known anyone like you."

"Did you think about her when you were fucking me?" I exhale in a rush. My mind is racing faster than my words will allow. "Did you look at me and imagine I was her?"

"Never," he snaps. "Don't say that. It's disgusting."

"You couldn't have her so you chose me to take her place," I push.

His grip firms and I tense from his touch. "I ache inside when I look at you, Alexa. You're so beautiful. You're the most beautiful woman I've ever met."

"I want to know why she's here," I say softly. Part of me wants to know. The other part doesn't know if it can shoulder the burden of the words. Once he tells me he's been screwing her, I have to accept it. He'll validate my worst fear. He's going to tell me that I crawled into the bed of a fucking liar again.

His hand leaps from my elbow before he pulls it into a knotted fist. "We can't talk about this right now. You have to go."

The dismissal bites through me. "I told you I wasn't leaving. Why did you bother planning a weekend away with me when you're still fucking her?"

His eyes rise from the floor and lock on mine. "I'm not fucking her." The words are clear and calm.

"Don't lie," I bark. "I saw her in that sheet. You had no clothes on. Why did you do it? Why?" The words all fall together in a messy heap as they leave my lips. There's no clear definition to them.

"Alexa, no." His hand is in the air now, waving aimlessly towards the hallway. "I didn't. I wouldn't touch her."

I steel myself against the words. How can he lie right to my face? Why is he lying? All I need to do is march down that hallway and confront her myself. "Where is she?" I take a few steps to the right but he's too quick. His hands grab my hips, pulling me back towards him.

"Don't do that." He takes a deep breath. "I'm serious. I need you to leave."

My eyes are transfixed on his face, studying his expression. It's a clear and uncompromising mixture of frustration and irritation. "I'm not going, Noah." I push against his chest, my hands resting on the firm bare skin.

"You're so fucking stubborn," he hisses the words out through clenched teeth as one of his hands leaps to my face. "Beautiful, stubborn, Alexa."

The rumble that is woven into my name pierces into me. I feel my body tighten at the sound. I don't want him to say my name. I don't want him to touch me. I just want to understand why a woman he claimed he didn't want is somewhere in this apartment, wrapped in one of his bed sheets. "Just tell me why, Noah."

He pulls his other hand to my face, cupping both my cheeks. "I didn't do anything with her. I don't want her."

"Why is she here?" I ignore what he just said. If I took any lesson away from my time with Brighton Beck it was that words pale in comparison to actions. Noah was nude when I go here, Camilla was practically nude. If I put two and two together that equals hot, crazy sex in his bedroom right before I arrived.

"Ari brought her." He doesn't elaborate beyond that. He just stares at me as if the mention of Arianna's name is going to open a floodgate of understanding.

"Is she here too?" I try to bend my neck in the direction of the hallway, but his grasp is too tight. The index finger of his right hand lazily runs over my cheekbone.

He only nods in response, his eyes piercing a dark path into me. I can sense the answers that I want are there, within my reach, but he's not going to offer them to me. He's shutting me out. He's gone from willingly wanting to board a train to explore New York City with me, to pulling back and inviting two women who both obviously want him into the penthouse retreat that he hides himself away in. What the fuck happened between yesterday and this minute? Why can't I ever get the happy ending that I want?

"I deserve better than this." I push against his hands with my own, but he's unyielding. "You said you wanted me." The words are a bitter whine that boils up from deep within me. They're laced with the beginnings of the tears that I feel welling up in my eyes. I haven't cried for more than a few minutes since I saw Brighton with Liz months ago. Now that image is tangled with the one of Noah and Camilla. I can't distinguish what's causing the immeasurable pain I'm feeling. Right now I hate them both. Correction, I hate all four of them.

"I agree." His thumb runs gently over my nose. "You deserve everything."

"I deserve an explanation," I bite back. "I deserve to know what the fuck is going on."

He moves forward until his chin is resting on my forehead. "You're right."

My breath stalls. This is when he confesses to fucking Camilla. This is the moment when he tells me that he saw her within my face and my body when I arrived weeks ago with that sandwich. He's going to tell me that he loves her and I was simply living on borrowed time until she reappeared. Why did I practically bash his door in to get back into this apartment? Why do I give a shit? I got over Brighton when he showed his true colors. I can do it again with Noah. I'm better than this.

"She had nowhere else to go," he whispers into my skin. "I couldn't let them live on the street."

"Them?" I push away harshly. I have to distance myself from him. I need to find those two women and give them a piece of my mind.

"Alexa." His tone is clipped as I race down the hallway, dropping my purse as I run.

I slow as I near the doorway to his bedroom and glance through. There's no one. I move towards the next room, grabbing onto the wall to steady myself as his large hands once again encircle my waist. I fall back into him as my gaze darts into the other bedroom. The blinds are partially drawn, only a small sliver of warm afternoon light pours into the space as my eyes meet Camilla's. My gaze travels down her face, towards the sheet still covering her body and the small bundled baby resting in her arms.

Chapter 2

"You have a baby?" My hand covers Noah's. I need him to answer the question. I need him to tell me whether the beautiful small gift that Camilla is cradling in her arms, is his child.

Camilla's eyes widen. "Obviously. Why is the delivery girl back?"

"Noah?" I can't turn to look at him. I'm so overcome with conflicting emotions. The baby is so tiny, so innocent and perfect.

"No, Alexa." He whispers the words as his lips feather over my ear. "It's not my baby."

I hold tightly to his hand as he pushes his chest against my back working to steady my balance. "Why then?" It's fragmented and breathy. I want to understand. I do. I want to comprehend why the woman he once killed for is sitting in a bed in his apartment with a newborn baby.

"Noah," Camilla looks past me directly to him. "Why is she here?"

"This is Alexa." He wraps his hands tighter around my waist, pulling me even closer to him. "This is the woman I told you about."

"The delivery girl is your girlfriend?" Her brow darts up with the same implied questions I have. "Why didn't you say something when she brought your food?"

Girlfriend. It's a word he's never spoken. We've never defined the connection between us, and hearing it from the lips of a woman who resembles me so closely is disorienting.

"Not girlfriend," he corrects. "She's my everything. She was my ..."

My breath stalls as his voice trails. "Was," I whisper in a heated rush. Something has changed.

"Alexa." His lips press against my hair. "We have to talk."

I've yet to turn to face him. I can't pry my eyes away from the sight of my almost twin and her baby. Why wouldn't he have told me Camilla had a child when I was asking about her days ago? Why keep that a secret? The knowledge that she'd had another man's child would have chased away all those doubts that have been plaguing me since I read her name in that text from Ari.

"What's she doing here?" As if on cue, Ari seemingly appears from out of nowhere. Her eyes blaze across my face as she pushes past Noah and I. "I brought you a snack." She hands an apple to Camilla before brushing her lips over the baby's forehead. "How's Abe?"

Abe. The baby is a boy. The disjointed pieces of the puzzle are being thrown together in a cluttered mess within my mind.

"Alexa is none of your business." Noah's hand jumps from my waist to my shoulder. "She's here to see me. Don't disturb us."

I don't resist as his hands pull me away from the door frame. I hear Arianna mutter something curse filled under her breath before we're out of ear shot.

"Come to my office."

Tears threaten and I take a heavy breath as he closes the door behind me. The fact that Camilla is here with a baby doesn't change the fact that Noah pushed me out of his apartment. He wanted me gone. He corrected himself when he called me his everything. This is over. The words haven't left his lips yet, but I can hear them coming. Noah Foster is going to break my heart. I can feel the splinters already.

"Sit down, Alexa." He reaches to pull my palm across his lips. I stare down at it, willing him to look me in the eye, but he won't.

I take a seat in the same leather chair that he carried in for me the other night when he was working. "Why are Camilla and her baby here?" Maybe if I stall long enough, he'll have a change of heart and he won't throw me out again. Maybe he'll remember how it feels to touch me, and laugh with me and live outside the confines of his insecurities.

"Her husband threw her out and changed the locks."

The word assaults me. *Husband?* Why had Camilla's husband and baby been such a secret before today? If Noah had only told me about them I wouldn't have wasted countless hours worrying about how she was going to swoop back in and steal him away from me.

"Camilla is married?" I ask with the ease of someone who is familiar with her. I'm not. I don't want to be. I don't care anything about Camilla or what her situation is. I care about Noah.

"I didn't know until the other day." He lowers himself into his desk chair, pulling on the fabric of his jeans. I can tell that he's uncomfortable.

That was only a few short days ago. Why does it feel as though the entire universe has shifted on its axis since then? I only nod as I wait for him to continue.

"Ari told me." He reaches for the arm of my chair, resting his elbow on it. "She told me Camilla was about to give birth and had been tossed out by her husband."

I push back into the soft leather of the chair to gain some distance from not only his body, but also his words. I don't know Camilla, but that hasn't stopped me from making assumptions about her. Regardless of how manipulative I might think she is, no one deserves to be shown the door right before they have a baby. "What kind of man does that?" My words are spotted with disgust.

"One who is fed up with his wife's bullshit," he says quietly. "She doesn't know who the father of her baby is." His gaze darts up to mine. "I'm not in the running. I haven't seen her for more than a year."

I feel an instant rush of relief bowl over me again. I believed him the first time he told me that the baby wasn't his, but the reassurance now is quelling my fears that there's more to their relationship than he's sharing. "How did she end up here? With you?" I add, strictly out of spite. I'm frustrated that my weekend with Noah crashed to a screeching halt because of his ex-girlfriend.

"Ari brought them over a few hours ago." He taps his finger against his upper lip. "Camilla wants to stay." He shakes his head as if to ward off the thought. "I'm having them moved to a hotel within the hour."

I take little comfort in the words. "Why did she say you two needed to talk before you threw me out?" I know the question is facetious. I'm still trying to absorb the fact that his ex looks identical to me.

"She wants to stay." A low chuckle rumbles through him. "That's not even an option."

"She was nude when I got here." I'm on a roll. I'm not about to stop with this line of questioning until I'm sure Camilla is out of the picture and his bed for good.

"She took off her top to feed him She's still wearing a skirt." He shrugs his shoulders. "I walked in on that and told her to shut the damn door before I had a shower."

The shower. "You were nude, Noah," I whisper. I'm so tired of him walking around naked in front of everyone. I get that it helps him deal with his scar and the insecurity that comes from that. I just don't get why he has to display his cock to everyone who steps foot in his apartment.

"I was on my way to my room to put on my pants." He slides his fist across his leg, smoothing out the denim fabric. "Camilla was out of the bedroom and answered the door before I could get to it."

"There's nothing going on between you two?" I cross my arms across my chest. "Nothing at all?"

"Nothing." He pulls the word slowly across his lips. "I told you I was done with her, Alexa. I meant it. I feel nothing for her. Nothing."

I feel a small smile tug at the corner of my lip. This is the first breath I've been able to fully take since I arrived, sandwich in hand, to pick him up for our New York getaway.

"Alexa?" His voice pulls me from my momentary bliss. "We need to be done too."

Chapter 3

"Why?" There's no masking the crack in my voice when I spit the question at him. "Why do we need to be done?"

He pushes back and stands. His fingers dart to his button fly as if he's about to undo his pants. He fidgets with the waistband before he pulls his hand into a fist. "Brighton was here this morning."

I nod impatiently. "I know. He told me." If Brighton Beck fucked this over for me, I'm going to hunt him down.

"When did he tell you?" He glares down at me. "When did you talk to him?"

"He came by my apartment before I came here." I don't want to talk about Brighton. I want Noah to get to the part where he's telling me it's over. There isn't a logical reason for that. Not after I just realized that he doesn't love his ex at all.

His eyes dart over my face for a minute before he finally speaks. "What did he say to you?"

"Why does it matter?" I snap back, my hand waving in the air. I'm beyond frustrated. I just want to get in a taxi and go to the train station so Noah and I can have a few days away from the rest of the world and all the people trying to come between the two of us.

His jaw tenses. "Did he tell you what we talked about?"

I hang my head in my palms. Brighton has done it again. He not only broke my heart in Paris, he's doing it again now in Boston. Why can't he just go to hell and stay there for the rest of my life? "He told me he was here, Noah. That's all he said."

"Alexa," he sighs before he walks across the room to stand in front of the photographs of my body. "He showed me some pictures."

"Pictures? What pictures?" I search my memory for any pictures of me that Brighton might have. Any he took of me were definitely G-rated. "I don't think he kept any pictures of me."

"He has dozens." Noah's back is to me now. His voice jumps across the walls and fills the silence in the room. "He showed me dozens."

I bolt to my feet. "What do you mean? What kind of pictures?"

He stares unflinchingly at the portraits on the wall. "Pictures of you smiling. Pictures of you in Paris."

I breathe out an audible sigh. "He took those when we were exploring the city together." There's no reason to deny that. Brighton and I spent days discovering the wonder of the city of lights hand-in-hand. I would have been smiling in most of those images. Back then I blindly believed everything he told me, including the fact that he was separated from his girlfriend, Liz.

"You have the most beautiful smile I've ever seen." He rubs his palm across his face, his fingers lingering briefly on the scar. "I couldn't stop staring at his phone. I must have scrolled through those photographs for an hour."

Brighton was here for an hour? What the hell happened between them? "If Brighton said anything about us still being together, he's a lying piece of shit."

Noah's head darts to the side, as he pulls his fingers to his lips. He bends his neck slightly so he can look directly at me. "He told me it's over. He made that clear."

The knot sitting in the pit of my stomach loosens slightly. "What is it then?" Whatever Noah thinks the problem is, I know that it's surmountable.

"I can't make you happy like that." He moves closer and brushes his lips slowly over my forehead. "I can't bring a smile like that to your face."

The words sting even though I know there's no reasoning behind them. I'm beginning to realize that I've never been happier than when I am with Noah. He makes me feel things no man ever has before. "You're wrong." That's all I can manage.

"Alexa." His hand darts out to reach for my cheek but it stalls less than a breath away. "I wanted to go to Manhattan with you. I know it was my idea. But..."

I don't wait for him to finish. "But nothing, Noah." I reach for his hand, pulling it to my face. I cover it with my own, pushing his skin into mine. "We don't have to go there. We don't have to go anywhere."

"In every one of those photographs on Brighton's phone you're so filled with joy." I hear the defeat in the words. His tone is different. It's not natural and confident. He's wavering. He actually believes that he can't make me as happy as Brighton. This is so messed up.

"Don't end this over some stupid pictures on Brighton's phone." I want the words to sound as flippant as the notion that is attached to them. I can't believe that Noah is going to dump me over some pictures that were taken months ago.

He turns on his heel now so he's facing me directly. His eyes float over my forehead before they skim across my cheeks and lock on my eyes. "It's not about the pictures, Alexa." His jaw tightens as my name leaves his lips. "It's about you."

"What about me?" I feel as though I've been thrown overboard into a rolling wave without any chance of a life preserver to help me ride the rapids. "I want to be with you." There's no need for subtlety at this point. Noah is going to break up with me before I even knew we were a couple.

His eyes widen a touch. "Your life is out there." His hand whips past my face towards the closed door of his office. "My life is in here." He bows his head towards the floor.

No. Please no. He was just beginning to come out of his shelter. Don't let what Brighton showed him take that away. Don't allow it to steal him away from me.

"We can stay here more." I push harder on his hand, willing him to cradle my cheek. I want a sign that he's not completely closed off.

"I can't do this, Alexa." He pauses. "I can never give you a full life."

I close my eyes, steeling myself for the onslaught of emotions. "Don't say that," I whisper. "Please, Noah, don't."

"I belong here." He pulls his hand free of mine. I instantly feel bereft at the loss of his touch.

"I belong here too," I say the words without thinking. They escape from the deepest part of me. I'm falling in love with him. I feel it now. I see it so clearly. "I want to be here with you."

He grazes his hands through his hair. "You can't," he whispers into the still, heavy air between us. "This has to end before it gets serious."

Before it gets serious? Really? We are way past the point of no return when it comes to serious. Is he fucking kidding me?

"I'm not going." I reach to grab hold of his forearms but he takes a heavy step back.

"I can't." His gaze carries past me to the wall. "I can't do this, Alexa."

I move slightly to the left trying to grab hold of his eyes with my own. "You're ending this because of those pictures Brighton showed you?" I have to find someone to blame for stealing my happiness away again. I know it's because of Brighton. He knew what seeing those pictures would do to Noah.

"I'm ending this because we can't make each other happy." He crosses his arms over his broad chest.

"We already do," I say, not caring that the words sound more like a clear plea than a solid statement. "You make me so happy."

"Your life is out there, Alexa." He nods towards the windows. "Go live it."

"I'm not going, Noah." I push on his chest. "Please don't end this. Please."

"Ari brought Camilla and Abe over just after Brighton left." He ignores my begging. "Abe's going to grow up one day and go to school, and play little league and have friends."

I feel as though the room is spinning. He's not making any sense. "What?"

"Camilla and whoever the hell she's with will take him out." He nods towards the bank of windows. "They'll take him out into the world that's out there."

"Who cares what Camilla does?"

"Alexa." He reaches up and runs his finger slowly along his scar. "I've thought about us non-stop for weeks. I've imagined my life with you."

I nod shamelessly. "I've imagined that too." I have. I've thought about what my life could be like if I gave my heart to Noah.

"I can't give you a life like that," he says hoarsely. "I can't give it to you or a child. If we got..."

My heart aches as the words trail. If we got married? If we got the chance to love each other? If we got to live our happy ever after?

"I'm ending this because I'm happy here and you're happy out there." The statement is definitive and calm.

"That's not true." I want to fall into him and help him see that I belong here, with him. He was just beginning to come out of his self-imposed cocoon when Brighton and Camilla showed up. How can he let those two people, who were so careless with our hearts, break our bond? "I know you care about me, Noah. I know that you do. Don't throw this away."

"Alexa." He takes a heavy step forward, his hands bolting to my face. "I'm not throwing this away."

"You are." I feel the sting of tears as I pull my arms around his waist. "Please don't, Noah. Please."

His lips graze slowly over my forehead. "I'm giving you a chance at the life you deserve," he whispers into my hair. "I want you to go live your life the way you're supposed to."

"I'm supposed to be here." I don't try and stop the sob. "I want to be here."

"I'll never forgive myself if I don't let you go." He clings tightly to my face. "I have to let you go."

I don't respond as he tilts my head up, looks me straight in the eyes and feathers his full lips over mine. "I'm falling in love with you, Alexa. This has to be goodbye."

"I'm falling …" the words get lost as he claims my mouth in a soft and tender kiss.

"Don't." He pulls back and stares at me, his face filled with pain. "Don't say it. Just go."

"I can't." I tug him closer, wanting to crawl inside his embrace. "Don't send me away."

His body tenses, his hands slide down to my shoulders and he pushes me away with his easy strength. "I can't do this. Please, Alexa, please just go."

My eyes glide over his chest, past the beautiful tattoos until they rest on his firm jaw. I close them briefly before I look into his eyes. "You're just upset about the pictures and Camilla showing up." I'm grasping for whatever wayward straws I can. "Don't end this over that."

"I knew I was getting too deep when I tried to go to your birthday party." He takes a heavy step back to gain distance. "I suggested New York because I thought I could do it. I knew it was what you wanted." His hands pull together in a tight viselike grip. "I've been panicked about it. I can't do it. I can't change just for you."

I recoil physically from the words. "I've never asked you to change, Noah."

"You kept pushing for me to leave here." He bows his head towards the floor. His hands run through his hair, messing it even more. "You weren't happy just being here with me."

I brush away the wayward blame he's trying to throw in my direction. "I wanted you to experience my life with me." It's true. All I wanted was for him to become a part of my life. "We don't have to go out anymore."

"You need to live out there." His hand glides over his chest. "I need to live in here."

"So that's it?" I ask quickly. "You're just going to throw us away like that?"

"I'm not throwing anything away." His response is clipped and bold. "I'm ending this before it gets more complicated."

I stare at him, marveling in how calm and collected he is in the face of this. "If I walk out, that's the end of it?" I'm not asking as much to gain his reaction, as to convince myself that this is actually the last time I'm going to look at his perfect face.

"Just go, Alexa." He points aimlessly in the direction of the door. "Don't look back. Go."

Chapter 4

"Did you tell Noah that you're moving to New York?"

It's been three months since I walked out of his apartment and each time someone has brought up his name it's speared through me like a hot torch. I've told Sadie that it's over between me and Noah Foster but she can't get her romantic mind to drop the idea of my happily-ever-after with him. Right now I just want to tell her to shut the hell up. "It's not any of his business." I actually say that calmly. How did I manage that?

"He'd want to know," she says sweetly.

He's been too busy ignoring my calls and text messages to care. I'd finally given up on trying to reach him two months ago. Since then I've been focused on building a new life, including finally graduating with my teaching degree. "He's got a lot going on." He's probably got it going on in his bed, on his couch and on the floor with a new round of blonde, blue eyed call girls.

"Why did you dump him?" She's not going to drop this. Maybe if I bring up Hunter she'll go all doe eyed on me and start waxing poetic about her husband.

"How's Hunter?" I pull his name slowly across my lips, enunciating each syllable as if I'm going to throw her into some sort of trance. "Did you thank him for giving me that part-time job at Axel NY?"

"We're pregnant." A slow smile carries over her lips as she brushes her long brown hair behind her ear. "We're having a baby."

"What the fuck are you talking about?" I feel my knees buckle and I instinctively grab the edge of the wooden headboard of my bed. "You're pregnant?"

Her sweet brown eyes fill with tears as she nods her head up and down. "I just found out today."

This is it. This is the point where my life and Sadie's separate forever. She's going to have a baby with Hunter and they'll complete their happy family and I'll move to New York into a two bedroom apartment with Kayla. My days will be filled with part-time substitute teacher work while I play waitress at Hunter's restaurant at night to cover my half of the rent. This is my life. It sucks. "I can't believe this." I can't believe any of it. My hands are shaking so hard that I fumble with the sweater I'm folding to pack into one of my suitcases.

"We don't know if it's a boy or girl yet." She runs her slim fingers over her flat belly. "Hunter is hoping for a girl. He didn't say that but he called the baby princess when I told him."

"You better hope to hell it's a girl." I wink at her. "Otherwise that baby boy in there is going to need a lifetime of therapy." My mind instinctively flips back to Noah's apartment and the image of Camilla holding Abe. I've struggled for months to absorb not only the fact that his ex looks like me, but that she had a baby and he willingly let her into his apartment before he threw me out onto the street.

"You'll come back when the baby is born, right?" She chirps the question out with a happy lilt running through her tone. I can hear the contentment in every syllable she speaks. She's found her place in the world. It's in Hunter's arms. I only wish I'd have had that chance with Noah too.

"I'll be back once a month to see you." My voice cracks slightly at the reminder that I won't get to visit her whenever I want. I've seen Sadie almost every day of my life, except for the months I was in Paris. Not being close to her is another change in my rapidly evolving world.

She leaps from my bed and onto her feet. "You can stay with Hunter and me. We have that extra room."

"You mean I don't have to sleep on the top bunk in Cory's room?" I playfully tease.

"Alexa." She reaches to pull me into a tight embrace. "I'm going to miss you like crazy."

"I'll miss you more," I whisper into her shoulder. "I'll miss you more than you know."

***

"There are so many hot guys in this city." Kayla scoops up a cardboard box from the entryway before she scurries down the hall towards her room.

I kick the edge of another box to determine its weight before reaching down to pull it into my arms. "I'm trying to avoid guys." I don't even have to say it. Kayla knows what happened between Noah and I. She listened to me whine about it all the way from Boston to New York yesterday.

"Just do one night stands." She tosses me a look as I walk into her bedroom. "You've had good luck with those."

"Just that one time." My mind lazily runs back to my first one night stand with Nathan. "It was fun."

"We should make a no relationship pact." She reaches for the box I'm holding. "These are my shoes." She plops it down onto her bed.

"What's a no relationship pact?" I tilt my head to the side, finally feeling a bit of the weight of the move leaving my shoulders.

"We just do guys one night at a time." She pulls the box open and starts throwing her shoes into the corner, each one bouncing against the wall before it lands on the floor. "We can fuck them and then move on."

I watch how carefree she looks as I consider the words. It was her idea to move here initially. She got a great job offer with a financial firm on Wall Street. After Noah dumped me she suggested I come along if I could find a job in the city. The best I could do was grabbing a spot on a list of substitute teachers. I was actually grateful when Hunter offered me a job at one of his restaurants here. Waitressing may not be my chosen career path at the moment, but it's going to pay my bills.

"It's a great plan. Right, Lex?" She's so bubbly and bright. It's no wonder. The last boyfriend she had was more than a year ago. She's better at this than I am. Her lust after them and then leave them philosophy may need to be my new motto.

"I guess," I offer.

"What about Beck?" The question comes so far out of left field that I almost feel an immediate sense of whiplash take over my brain.

"Beck?" I've avoided talking to her about him. When I finally got him to speak to me a few weeks ago on the phone after calling him incessantly, he claimed he was only trying to reassure Noah that he was over me by showing him those pictures before he deleted them. I'd called him out of his obvious bullshit and then he abruptly ended the call after telling me he'd love me forever. If Beck's idea of love is the only thing I can get, I'll happily stay single for the rest of my life.

She pushes the now empty cardboard box off her bed. "You said on the train that he was the reason Noah dumped you."

The words still bite, even more so coming from the mouth of someone else. "Noah said that Brighton showed him pictures of us together," I repeat almost word-for-word what I told her during my never ending confession about what happened in Noah's apartment that afternoon. "I think Brighton did it because he knows Noah is insecure."

"Maybe Noah was using it as an excuse because he was having second thoughts about his ex."

It's not a foreign thought to me so I don't reject the idea immediately. "I've thought about that too." I settle onto a corner of the bed. "Noah said he was moving Camilla to a hotel that day."

"How do you know that even happened?" She tips her chin in my direction. "You took his word for it."

"He wasn't lying." I don't think he was lying. He had no reason to lie.

"Maybe they're all one big happy family right now. Maybe Beck did you a favor."

My stomach recoils at the thought of Noah building a life with Camilla and Abe. "I want to believe what he told me," I whisper. "I want to believe that he ended it because he wanted me to be happy."

"I don't think you'll ever know for sure." She shrugs her shoulders as she rounds the bed. "It's water under the bridge now. Noah Foster is your past."

I nod as I watch her hurry through the door. I listen as her footsteps pad along the hardwood floor back towards the foyer.

Chapter 5

"I'm Jessica." One of the sous chefs reaches out her hand to grab mine. "It's great to meet you, Alexa."

I smile warmly at her. After arriving an hour ago to Axel NY with Hunter in tow, I'd been given the red carpet treatment. I'd joked with him that he was going to make my life a living hell by broadcasting to the entire staff that I was a personal friend. The quick, friendly hug he gave me in response was welcome. I'd been in New York a week now and everything still felt completely alien to me.

"It's nice to meet you too." I shake her hand carefully, studying her face. She's beautiful. Her blue eyes a slightly deeper shade than mine, her blond hair pulled back tightly into a bun. Her features are sculpted. She could have been a model if she wanted, save for the fact that she's slightly shorter than me.

"You'll love it here." Her smile beams past me towards where Hunter is standing next to us. "Hunter's management team is the best."

I wish I could join in her enthusiasm for the job, but truth be told, I haven't waitressed since high school. My job at Star Bistro back in Boston may have included waiting on people, but it's a much different experience being a barista. This job was going to mean long nights on my feet, lots of rich, spoiled customers and no special treatment. Hunter made it clear to me, before I left for Boston, that he expected a lot out of me. He also confided in me, that tips, on the nights he scheduled me for, were the absolute best. Maybe he was as good of a guy as Sadie made him out to be.

"Alexa is a very old friend of my wife's," Hunter says as he reaches to rest his hand on my shoulder. "She needs to go through the same process as everyone else though. Don't hold back."

Jessica laughs before she pulls her hand over her mouth. "I'll do my best to help her get the groove of the place."

"Thank you," I mouth under my breath.

"Alexa." Hunter's hand glides to my elbow. "Let's talk about your schedule over here."

"How's Sadie feeling?" I look down at the floor. "I'm sorry I haven't called her yet."

"Sadie's fine." His voice is deep and smooth. "Noah Foster called Axel looking for you."

My stomach knots as I feel a flash of hope race through me. "Axel Boston?" It's an obvious question that is biding me time. I've waited three months to hear that Noah wanted to talk to me. Now that it's a reality I need time to process it.

"Two nights ago," he offers. "He called twice. Bernie ended up delivering the sandwich."

My eyes dart up. I want to ask for Bernie's number so I can drill him with questions. "Did he ask about me?"

"Yes." I see the concern in his face. "I spoke to him the second time he called. I told him you'd moved."

"Did you tell him where?" The rush of giddiness that is sweeping through me is intoxicating. This is what I've waited months for. A sign from Noah that we might still have a future.

"Alexa." Hunter leans forward grabbing both my shoulders in his hands. "I'm only telling you this because you have a right to know."

"Tell me exactly what he said." I want every detail. I want him to repeat every single syllable that Noah uttered to him. I want to know it all.

"He asked if you could bring him a sandwich. The hostess who initially took his call said Bernie would deliver it."

I nod heavily. So far, so good. Noah called looking for me. That has to mean something.

"He called back and I answered." He exhales audibly, his brow furrowing. "I told him you were unavailable."

My heart sinks at that confession but why wouldn't Hunter tell him that? I've moved to another state. It wasn't as if I could jump on a train and rush back to deliver his food for him. "What did he say?"

"He asked me when you'd be available." He looks past my shoulder towards someone who has called his name. I watch him nod slowly.

"Did you tell him I was here?" I point to the floor. "Did you tell him I was in New York?"

"I told him you moved."

"To New York?" I push. I'm getting impatient. I want Hunter to tell me that he gave Noah directions to my apartment here. I want him to be waiting on my stoop when I walk home tonight.

"He asked if you moved to Paris."

"Paris?" The question comes out with as much surprise in the word as I feel inside. "What did you tell him?"

"I said it wasn't Paris and..." he stops to take in a heavy breath.

"And what, Hunter?" I look right into his eyes. "Did you tell him I was here?"

"He hung up before I could tell him anything." He closes his eyes briefly as if he's warding off the pain he knows I'm feeling.

"What about Bernie?" I scrub my hands over my face. "Did he talk to Bernie about me?"

"Alexa." His voice is low and soft. "You need to forget about him."

"Tell me, Hunter." I hear the unmistakable crack of approaching tears in my voice. I've held everything in since Noah pushed me out of his apartment twice in one night. Holding it together now is quickly becoming impossible. "What did he say to Bernie?"

His eyes reach into mine and I see compassion there. It's misplaced. Hunter and I aren't friends. He's an extension of my relationship with Sadie. That's it. I don't want him to feel pity for me. I don't want him to offer me anything but the truth. "Bernie didn't see Noah."

"What do you mean?"

"A woman answered the door and took the sandwich from him."

Chapter 6

"It's just guilt." Kayla runs her finger along the menu of the small diner she chose for our Wednesday afternoon late lunch. "All guys have it after they dump you."

"What?" I raise a brow over my menu to stare at her. "What are you talking about?"

"I'm having a bowl of soup. It's so cold today." She pulls the knitted grey sweater she's wearing around her shoulders. "What do you want?"

"The same," I say without thinking. I haven't had any appetite at all since Hunter told me about Noah two days ago. I'd kept that information to myself. Kayla is too quick to offer her opinion on why men do the things they do. I'd held onto the knowledge that Noah had been looking for me because I wanted the hope that it offered. I'd conveniently tried to ignore the fact that a woman had answered the door. It didn't matter if it was Camilla, Ari or a call girl at this point. Noah had someone else with him.

"When a man dumps a woman guilt starts to set in at about the two month mark," she says it so matter-of-factly. "You two split up months ago so it makes sense that he's checking up on you. He wants that guilt to go away. He's just making sure you're happy."

This is exactly why I didn't want to tell her about Noah. I didn't want her to deflate the emotional balloon I've been carrying around since Monday. "I don't think that's the reason every guy wants to talk to his ex."

"Did you try calling him after Hunter told you?"

I had. Twice. Both times it went straight to voicemail. I didn't know what to say, so I'd hung up without leaving a message. "Yes," I confess. Lying to Kayla isn't going to help me in the least. If anything, being truthful with her will slap me back into reality. Holding out false hope for a bittersweet reunion with Noah isn't doing my heart an ounce of good.

"What?" She drops the menu into the middle of the table, almost knocking my water glass over. "What did he say?"

"Nothing," I spit back. "He didn't answer."

"There's your answer right there." She motions over my head towards the waiter. "If he wanted you back, he'd have answered, or at the very least, he would have called back when he noticed your number."

I'd told myself that for a hot second before I latched onto every other conceivable reason for why Noah hadn't answered or called me. "He doesn't want me back, does it?"

"Lex." She leans over the table, cupping her hand over mine. "It's guilt. That's it. You've got to forget about him."

She's right. As much as I don't want to admit that she's got it all figured out, she does. Noah Foster would have called my number if he wanted to talk to me. That says more than a request for a sandwich ever could.

***

"You should go out to dinner with me." A deep, melodic voice caresses my ear from behind. I almost drop the plates I'm carrying over to the middle-aged couple who can't seem to keep their hands off each other. Hopefully, in all of their teenage like bliss, they will at least leave me a decent tip. They haven't stopped staring lovingly into each other's eyes since they arrived.

I spin around on my heel. My breath catches at the sight of a dark haired man with striking green eyes. His tall frame is covered in a tailored grey suit. His eyes course over my body and I instantly wish I wasn't wearing the required white button up blouse and black skirt that every waitress here is dressed in. Maybe New York isn't so bad after all. "Excuse me?" I may have misheard him in all the hustle and bustle of the jam packed space. It's Friday night, which means that the reservation list is full and people's wallets are easily emptied. I can effortlessly make a few hundred dollars tonight in tips if I keep my eye on the prize. That means I can't chit chat with the suit too long.

"Do you want to have dinner with me?" The corner of his mouth perks up revealing a set of perfect white teeth.

"I can stop by occasionally while you eat dinner," I tease, motioning to one empty table in the corner. "I'm sorry but I'm very busy."

"I'm Alec." He holds out his hand with a nod of his head. "You're Alexa."

I smile at the knowledge that he's asked someone for my name. This isn't like Star Bistro where any guy who wanted to flirt could start by reading my name off my name tag. "You've asked about me." It's a statement, not a question. I'll play his little game for twenty seconds more.

"How could I not?" His hand hangs in the air between us. I nod towards the two still warm plates in my hands.

"I'm sorry, Alec," I say softly. "I need to get back to work."

"I'll wait." He motions towards the empty table. "I'm over there."

I raise a brow before turning on my heel. My plan to get over Noah Foster may just be seated at table twenty-eight.

Chapter 7

"He's not Noah," I whisper under my breath as I brush my long hair.

"That's a good thing, Lex," Kayla holds up a black sleeveless dress she's pulled from her closet. "This one would be killer."

I shake my head. "It's too short. I'm a grade school substitute teacher now. I can't have everything hanging out for the entire world to see."

She laughs a little too hard. "It's not that short. I wear it all the time."

I cock a brow in response. Kayla has been out every night this week when I'd gotten home from the restaurant. She is definitely enjoying the party life of a single woman in Manhattan. I, on the other hand, am waiting with baited breath for Noah to call Hunter back to ask for another sandwich. Every single day when I speak with Sadie it's the first question out of my mouth. Every single day I get the same answer and that's there's been no orders from Noah since that one night.

"This one then?" She holds up a navy blue shift dress that is cut just above the knee. "You'd look like a bombshell in this one."

I nod. Agreeing to have dinner tomorrow night with Alec is a decision I've been questioning since I sat down at his table during my break. He is charming, seductive and gorgeous. He is also the owner of a successful start-up, twenty-nine and single. He is everything any woman could want. The problem is that I need to get my mind wrapped around the fact that this is how I'm going to move forward and leave Noah Foster behind me.

"It's been almost four months now, Lex." Kayla lays the dress carefully in my lap. "You've been apart longer than you were together. Get over it."

I stop to consider the words. She's absolutely right. Noah and I dated inside his apartment for a short time. If he wanted me back, he would have come looking for me by now. "I never thought about it that way," I say honestly. "You're right."

"Of course I am." She laughs. "You have the night off tomorrow. You're going to wear that dress, knock Alec off his socks and hopefully you'll land right in his bed."

I run my hands over the dress, look up into her eyes and wink. "Alexa Jackson is back. Alec has no idea what's headed his way."

***

"A teacher?" His jaw tenses. "I thought you were a waitress."

Who would have thought that any man would be put off by the thought of dating a teacher? Doesn't that rank somewhere in the top ten of what men fantasize about? "I'm both."

"So you work here at night and at school during the day?"

Is that a hint of interest in his voice? "I'm a substitute teacher so I'm there when they need me and I work four nights a week here."

"Have you ever dined here before?" He tips his glass of wine in my direction.

"Several times." I look past his head to smile at one of my co-workers. "The owners are close friends of mine."

"You know Hunter?" His face lights up. "Hunter and I go way back."

"Way back where?" I question. "Hunter's pretty tight lipped about his glory days before he met his wife."

"Sadie." Her name flows across his lips with such ease. Who knew that Alec would know my best friend?

"Sadie and I have been best friends since grade school." I run my tongue over my lower lip, suddenly feeling parched. I haven't had a conversation with any attractive man beyond taking his order, since I arrived in New York. Now, I'm in the company of one who not only knows Hunter, but he's met Sadie too.

"Shut the hell up." He blurts the words out and they feel misplaced coming from someone so smooth and cultured. "I can't believe you know them."

"I knew them first," I tease. "I win."

"I've known Hunter just as long." He cocks a brow. "You haven't won anything yet."

"What's the prize?" I lean forward just a touch.

"Something you'll never forget."

I close my eyes briefly as his hand reaches across the table to touch my chin. It's strong, warm, and beneath his touch is an unmistakable sensual grace. "You win," I whisper.

"Alexa?" A woman's voice pulls me from my thoughts and my eyes dart to the side. It's Jane, the front of the house manager. "I'm sorry to bother you on your night off, but there's something…" she stalls as her eyes lock on Alec. "There's just an issue that we need to talk about. I need your help with something."

What the fuck? I'm a waitress. I have absolutely no say in anything that goes on in this restaurant. What the hell does she need from me and why now? Why does this have to happen when I've got a massively attractive man with a ready, willing and probably impressive dick just waiting to take me home to fuck me senseless?

"What?" I blurt the word out with all the unmitigated annoyance I feel inside. "What is it?"

"Can I borrow you for a brief moment?" She gestures towards a corner to the side.

"I guess." I shrug my shoulders at Alec, hoping that he's not going to change a thing about what he wants while I'm in the corner talking about whatever the hell Jane thinks can't wait. If this is about my schedule, I'm going to pull the Hunter Reynolds card out of my pocket and scare her shitless. Her timing couldn't have been any worse if she planned it on cue.

"I'll be right here." Alec offers while he gestures for the waiter. "I'll have another drink."

I pick up my clutch, remembering the mantra my mother drilled into my head before I went out on my first date. "*Never leave your purse alone, Lexie. You never know when a hoodlum will steal it.*"

"What is it, Jane?" I say with frustration. "I'm on a date."

"A man keeps calling." She shuffles back and forth on her feet. "It sounds like a prank but he knows your name."

My stomach flips before it flops. "A man?"

"He wants a smoked brisket on rye." She shakes her head. "We don't serve those sandwiches here. They do at the location in Boston. I tried to get him to order something else, but he said he wants that and he wants you to bring it to him."

I can't breathe. My heart is pounding so loud I can't hear anything else in the room. "Give me the address. Give it to me."

Chapter 8

I stall just as I'm about to knock on the door. The address is on the Upper East Side in a pre-war building. It had taken me all of a minute to grab the small piece of paper from Jane's hand, run by Alec to tell him I was sorry and hail a taxi to bring me here; to bring me to Noah. I'd arrived five minutes ago but I spent the majority of those rehearsing what I want to say to him.

The door swings open. Before I have a chance to react he's pulling me inside. His massive hands circling my waist, his face buried in my hair. I claw at his arms. The silence only broken by the dull thud of the door as he kicks it shut behind us.

"God, Alexa. God," he whispers into my hair. "I've missed you. I've missed you," he repeats in a low voice. "Every day has been torture."

I try to break free so I can look at him. My gaze is cast down out of necessity. My eyes catching on the black dress slacks he's wearing and his bare feet. "Noah." My voice is lost in his chest.

He pulls back slightly, his hands darting to my face. I feel the warmth of them as he guides my face up to meet his. I take in every curve, relishing in the sight of his familiar chin, the strength of his brow and the beauty of his scar.

"You're so perfect." His eyes tear a path across my face, stopping to study each of my features. "I've missed your beautiful face."

I can't take my eyes off of him. I feel as though I've stepped into a dream. "You're here."

"I came here for you." He brushes his lips across my forehead. "I came to find you."

"How did you know I'd be here?"

I feel his lips feather over my cheek before they brush across mine. "I called Axel Boston and someone there told me you were in Manhattan." He stops to kiss me lightly again. "She told me you were working at the restaurant here."

"I tried to call you." My hands move from his waist to his hands, pushing them closer into my face. I've been starved for his touch for months. I finally feel as though I can breathe again. "I called you a few weeks ago. You didn't call me back."

"I didn't know what to say." His eyes glisten slightly and I know that he's feeling everything I am. "I just wanted to see you. I wanted to hold you and look at you."

"So you came to New York?" I nod my head towards the floor. "You came here to see me?"

"Yes." His eyes dart from my eyes to my mouth and back again. "I came here to see you."

I have a million questions but I can't form a single one. I can only stare at him.

"You look so beautiful." His eyes skim over my dress. "You were out tonight, weren't you?"

I nod. I've never lied to Noah. Starting now seems foolish. "I was on a date. I was at the restaurant when you called."

"Is he important to you?" There's no anger or jealousy woven into the question at all. It's direct.

I shake my head slightly from side-to-side. "I just met him. We hadn't even ordered yet."

"Tonight was your first date?" This time there's no hiding the emotion in the question. He's happy. I can sense it between the words.

"My first date since I got here," I offer.

"Then I got here just in time." His hands tangle in my hair, pulling my mouth into his for a lush, deep kiss.

My eyes flutter closed as I lose myself in the touch in the man that I'm in love with. There's absolutely no question of that within any part of me now. I love Noah Foster. I belong with Noah Foster. Now I just need to make that my reality.

***

"I got a new tattoo." He's sitting on the edge of the coffee table, my bare feet resting between his thighs, which are still hidden beneath the fabric of his pants. "I got it right after you left."

I want to correct him. I want to tell him that I didn't leave. At least, I didn't leave willingly. In his effort to force me into the world that he thought would make me happy, he abandoned me in many ways. I'm not over that. I can't be. I have so much I need to say to him. "Where?" I ask the obvious question for now.

"Here." His hand darts to his chest. It rests directly over his heart.

"I can't see." I lean forward, all the while painfully aware that my breasts are about to dive out of the top of Kayla's dress. It's just a touch too small but that hadn't stopped me from squeezing myself into it earlier in an effort to impress Alec. I had no idea that hours later, I'd be sitting with Noah, staring at his beautiful chest.

"Right here." His finger traces a small space in the middle of a larger tattoo. "It's the numbers six and seventeen."

"Is that a combination to something?" I laugh expecting him to follow suit. I tone it down the moment I realize his expression is stoic and serious.

"It's the day we met." His voice is low and tender.

It's a gesture that I wasn't expecting. "When did you get this?" I rest my hand over it, closing my eyes to bask in the firmness of his body. He's all muscle. He radiates power and control.

"The night you left." His hand covers mine now. "I went and had it done right away to remind myself of you."

"I didn't leave, Noah." I can't stomach hearing him say those words to me. I've been living in pained agony for months because he chose to turn his back on my world and me, in favor of the world within the walls of his apartment.

"I know, Alexa." He moves forward, pulling my legs so I skim my ass across the couch. "I pushed you away. I've had to live with that every moment of every single day. I can't take it anymore."

Chapter 9

"Your body is so fucking perfect, Alexa." He glides his tongue over my thigh. "I've ached inside thinking about this body."

I lean my head back into the pillow on the king size bed as he slides his mouth over my folds. I moan loudly, relishing in the feeling, wanting it to last forever. "Noah, please, lick it like that."

"You want to come like this, don't you?" He circles my clit with painfully slow strokes of his tongue. "Your pussy is so good."

"Make me come," I'm almost begging. "I want this."

He pushes my thighs farther apart as he moves his head quickly back and forth, mirroring the efforts of his tongue. He brings me to the edge smoothly. He knows exactly how to lick, touch and fuck my body until I'm screaming his name over and over again.

"I'm so close," I scream as I tangle my hands in his hair. "Yes, Noah."

"Come for me," he breathes into my wetness, his breath skirting hot over the sensitive tissues. "Come now."

The growl deep within his voice pushes me into an intense orgasm. My legs try to move out of sheer reflex from the heat pouring through my skin. He holds tight to them, his lips centered on my core, trying to coax another orgasm from me.

"No, Noah," I beg. "It's too much."

"Never," he purrs as he sucks my swollen bud between his lips and I pull hard on his hair, screaming out as I fall into the depth of pleasure yet again.

"I can't," I whimper as I hear him tear the foil packet of the condom package. "I can't."

"I need to fuck you." He hoists my left leg up, adjusting my body to take his full length. He slides in with urgency, his full, thick cock filling me instantly. He leans forward, his lips taking mine into a deep, soul touching kiss. His body is still, the only movement his tongue as it parts my lips.

I moan into his mouth. I want him to fuck me. I want to watch his gorgeous face as he chases his own orgasm within my body. "Fuck me, Noah," I whisper softly against his lips. "Just fuck me."

He pulls back. His breath touches my cheek. I feel a drop before I see it. There are tears silently falling from his eyes. "I love you, Alexa. I love you."

I don't speak. I can't. I can only feel as he pushes back on his knees, raises himself up on his hands, and fucks me hard and slow until he lets out a guttural groan.

***

"That's the Noah I remember," I say with a small smile as he comes walking back into the bedroom completely naked with two bottles of chilled water.

"You've missed my cock." He points down to his groin. He's still semi-erect. "I don't blame you."

I laugh at the words. "I've missed you."

"I keep it covered more now." He loosens the cap on one bottle before handing it to me. "You were right. I needed to put on some pants."

"In public?" I cock a brow as I take a lazy, large swallow of the water. "Or in private?"

"I'm almost always alone." He brings the bottle in his hand to his mouth. "I like looking at my dick, so I don't wear pants when it's just me."

I almost spit water all over the bed. "It's a nice dick." I shrug one shoulder. "I like it."

"You love it," he teases. We both ignore the obvious emotional elephant in the room. Since Noah had tenderly told me he loved me, I'd remained mum on the subject. I can't say those words to him tonight. I need to understand what happened all those months ago in his apartment. I also need to understand what's happened in his life since then, including what's going on with Camilla and the baby.

"When did you get here?" It's a good starting point.

"A week ago." He doesn't offer more and there's no indecision in the words. He's been in Manhattan an entire week and hasn't reached out.

"You got here last week?" I repeat it back. It's not that I expect it will have a different meaning coming from my lips. I just want clear understanding of what his motivations are and why it took him so long to get in touch. "Did you come because of your work?"

He raises a brow before taking another large sip from the bottle. "I came here for you, Alexa."

"Why did you wait so long to get in touch?"

"I saw you the first day I was here." He places the bottle on the night stand before reaching for my hand.

I shift my body slightly, pulling the sheet around my frame. I don't want to feel completely exposed when we talk about this. I need a barrier between us, and knowing Noah, he isn't about to cover up anything that is already on full display. "Why didn't you say something?"

His hand bolts to his chest to cover the new tattoo. "I wanted to see how you were. I wanted to see if you were…"

"If I was happy?" I interrupt. We are actually going to dive right back into the one subject that broke us up. Maybe this reunion is going to be short lived, after all.

"If you were happy," he parrots back. "You are happy."

"That depends on how you define happy, I suppose. " My mouth tightens. "I've missed you like crazy, Noah. I've missed you so much."

"We need to talk about things." He's on his feet now. "I want to know about your life here. I want to know what you're doing. How is teaching?"

I nod. "We need to talk about all of that."

He stands in silence, his hands resting on his strong hips. "Let's start with Brighton."

I curse inwardly. We are actually going to jump back onto the merry-go-round that is Brighton Beck's role in my life? "Why?"

"He's here." Noah taps his index finger against his hip bone. "Brighton is in New York."

Chapter 10

"I haven't seen him." I pull my gaze back down to the sheets. "I haven't spoken to him in months."

"He said you called him about what happened that day in my apartment."

I nod my head. "I did. I wanted to find out why he showed you the pictures, Noah."

He fidgets from one foot to the other. "I hate that you loved him."

I smile at the confession. I pull my gaze up to meet his. "I hate that I loved him too," I say the words clearly and slowly so there's no room for misinterpretation between them.

"I think about it sometimes." His voice cracks slightly. "I think about you being in his arms. How he must have felt when he was inside you."

I exhale sharply. "I don't even remember it." I'm not lying. Intimacy with Beck was lovely at the time. I know I enjoyed it. I know that it filled an empty need within me that was swallowing me whole back then. I was so lost in Paris. I felt so alone and Brighton was there. He felt like home. I needed that.

"You don't?" It's a misplaced question on his lips. Noah has never outwardly shown any real jealousy. He may have gotten irritated with Brighton when he realized we were once lovers, but he's always been confident in our connection. I've felt that right from the start.

"When I was in Paris," I begin before I pat the bed willing him to sit down next to me. He does. "When I was in Paris, I felt very lost."

"You went there alone, didn't you?" He pulls the sheet over to reveal my leg. "Were you running away from something here?"

"Someone you mean?" I know Noah well enough to realize that he's asking me if I left home because of a man.

He nods slowly as his finger traces a path along my calf. "Were you involved with someone before Paris?"

"No." I shake my head from side-to-side. "I didn't date anyone for long." I steel my breathing. I want to tell him about the girl I used to be. I want him to understand who I was then and who I am now. "I was mostly interested in men for sex."

He cocks a brow as the corner of his mouth twitches. "You fucked around?"

"I did." Why try and hide the fact that I used to be that girl? I was the one who would hook up with a man just because I needed to feel that rush of pleasure. "I was safe and sane about it." I close my eyes to ward off the many faces of the men I've randomly fucked over the years. "I didn't want anything serious."

"Do you think you ran to Paris to escape that?" It's a serious question that requires an honest answer.

"Sadie fell in love with her husband around that time." I cringe inwardly thinking about how I felt knowing my best friend had fallen into the lap of the man of her dreams, while I was jumping from bed-to-bed searching for anything that could satiate my needs that day. "I saw how happy she was. I wanted that too."

"You moved all the way to Paris to get that?" His fingers trace a path around each of my toes.

"I moved to Paris so I could be with myself." I've never confessed this to anyone, not even Sadie. "I didn't like who I was. I was always searching for the next party or club to go to. I couldn't be alone with myself for more than a few hours."

"Why?" I see the genuine concern in his eyes.

"I wanted to be a girl that men fell in love with too." It's a direct confession that leaves me wide open and vulnerable. "I wanted a man to stay with me beyond one night."

"Alexa," he whispers my name as he crawls up the bed. "How could any man not want to be with you forever?"

I sigh heavily. "I would give my number to men after we'd hooked up." I pull my gaze from his, embarrassed by the words about to leave my lips. "They wouldn't call."

"What?" He jumps back onto his knees so he's facing me directly. "What the fuck was wrong with them?"

I laugh at the animated tone in his voice. "They knew I'd put out. They got what they wanted." Honesty is the best policy, right? It had taken me weeks after leaving Boston for Paris before I realized any of this. The time I'd spent alone there, pre-Beck was a period of gentle awakening for me. I'd cried for hours thinking about where my life was. I'd planned for days on where I wanted to be in a year, in five years and in ten years.

"How did Brighton enter the picture?" I knew the question was coming. It was settled, simmering on the back burner, waiting for the moment when it would need Noah's full attention again.

I look into his eyes. I need him to fully understand the bare honesty that is woven into my words. "He saved me when I was lost." The words carry a double meaning.

"You told me months ago that you shared a mutual friend?"

"It's the man who owns the restaurants." I push my leg closer to Noah, longing for his continued soft touch. "He's Sadie's husband."

Noah massages the sole of my foot. His strong hands deftly push into the skin, pulling out the stress and pain that has settled there after all the long nights I've spent on my feet at the restaurant lately. "They connected you with Brighton?"

"I was lost one day and they had given me his number." I push back the memory of that day and the first glimpse I had of Brighton's face. "He helped me find my way out of the maze that is the streets of Paris." I smile softly. "We went for a coffee and talked for hours."

"You fell fast for him?"

"Very," I say, not looking at him. "We bonded quickly."

"You didn't know about his girlfriend?" A brief glimpse of something skirts across his gaze. "About Liz?"

"Sadie told me he had gone there to help her after an accident." I continue," I asked him about her that first day. It was while we were drinking our coffee. He told me they weren't together anymore. He said that he was there working and helping her if she needed him."

He studies my profile. I can feel his eyes boring into me. "You believed him?"

"Why wouldn't I?" I spit back, trying not to sound as defensive as I feel. I've questioned myself endlessly about my decision to put that much faith in Brighton.

He bites his lip. His hands stall briefly before he exhales audibly. "He wanted you the moment he saw you. He told me. He would have said anything to be with you."

I berate myself silently each day for getting involved with Brighton. "I'll never get rid of the guilt," I say softly. "I'll never shake off that feeling that I fucked up the life of his girlfriend."

"You didn't." He leans down to circle my legs with his arms, resting his head against my thighs. "He did that. You just loved him."

Chapter 11

"He's here? He's in New York?" Kayla bounces across the kitchen floor towards me. I almost feel the need to duck under the table for cover.

"Yes," I answer trying not to sound as annoyed as I do. "Beck is here."

"Are you going to see him?"

"No," I spit back a little too harshly. "I don't want to. I doubt that he wants to see me."

"I think you should see him." She pours a healthy dose of milk into her coffee. "I think you should give him a piece of your mind for the way he fucked up everything with Noah."

I roll my eyes, before reaching to pop two pieces of grain bread into the toaster. "You haven't listened to anything I've told you." I'm frustrated. She has to know that. We've sat here for the past twenty minutes while I rambled on incessantly about how Noah is in New York. The quiet mention of Brighton was only to move the story along. I didn't know she'd focus on it, and it, alone.

"I have so." She stomps her foot like a contemptuous two-year old child. "You said that Noah came to New York to see you and that Brighton is here too."

"I won't see Beck," I'm saying it as much for my own benefit, as hers. "I can't open that door again. I have nothing left to say to him."

She sips at her coffee. "He hasn't tried to contact you, Lex. Maybe he's not here to see you."

"You're right." I feel an instant weight drift off my shoulders. If Brighton wanted to see me, he would have found me by now.

"What about Noah?" She points to the toaster. "What happened with you two?"

I reach for the toasted bread, handing one slice to her. "Do you want jam or anything?"

"Nothing," she says as she munches on the very dry corner. "Tell me about Noah."

"He mostly wanted to talk." I don't look her in the eye. I focus instead on pushing my toast to the corner of my plate. "He wanted to talk about Brighton." I conveniently leave out the part where Noah said he loves me.

""What's with that?" She takes another sip from the mug. "He talks about Brighton more than you do."

I've had the same thought but my mind has tried to bury it in its dark recesses, just as I did with the sight of Camilla wrapped in a bed sheet. "I wanted to talk about other things."

"Why didn't you?"

It's a valid question. After Noah and I had played twenty question of Brighton Beck, he'd gone down to the street with me to hail me a cab home. I had wanted to stay to wrap myself around him for the night but he said it was late and he wanted time to rest. It was a brush off that still stung now, eight hours later. "He was tired." It sounds even lamer coming out of my mouth than it did when it was just drifting around in my mind.

"You haven't seen each other in months and he sends you home?" She shakes her head as she chuckles softly. "What's with that dude, Lex? Seriously, what's his deal?"

I take a small bite of toast to avoid having to answer that somewhat rhetorical question. I have no idea what his deal is but I need to find out before my heart starts reinvesting itself in him.

***

"I might get a permanent placement at a school in Queens next fall." I tuck my legs under me as I watch Noah move seamlessly across the room.

"Are you sure you don't want anything to drink?" He tips the open bottle of beer in his hand in my direction. "I can make you something warm." The suggestion is misplaced considering he's nude from the waist up. This is now the second time I've arrived at this apartment to find him wearing pants. This time it's jeans.

"Is this a short term rental?" It's a question I've had perched at the edge of my lips since I realized he was in New York. The apartment is large and beautifully decorated.

"It's mine," he says it with ease. "It's my father's actually but he's in China right now."

I survey the details of the space more closely, soaking in the rich details of the ornate furniture, the beautifully woven rugs on the floors and the artwork that hangs proudly on display. "Are you staying in New York long?"

He puts the bottle of beer on the coffee table before he sits down next to me. "I'll stay here as long as you do."

The words hit me with the full force of a speeding freight train. My hand jumps to my chest to level my breathing. "You're staying in New York?"

"I'm not going back to Boston." It's a twisted answer to a simple question. "Why would I go back there now? If you've got a job lined up, I'm here to stay."

Any lingering doubts I may have had about Camilla have been quashed like a tiny mouse racing across the path of a cat. "You work in Boston."

"I can't work." He doesn't show an ounce of emotion as the words leave his lips. "I don't want to take nude photographs anymore."

"What?" That's his thing. It's what he does. I can't level my breathing enough to disguise the pure joy that I feel knowing that he's not bouncing naked on a bed with a nude blonde call girl in his lens finder anymore. "What will you do?"

"I'll take pictures of you." He nods his head towards my body, which is still fully clothed. "I could take pictures of you forever, Alexa."

I blush at the reminder of the row of photographs he has lining the wall of his office back in Boston. "You can't make a living taking pictures of me."

"I'll live on sandwiches for the rest of my life then. They're cheap."

I giggle at the notion, knowing that sandwiches are his least favorite thing. "You're charming, Noah Foster."

He shakes his head slightly as his right brow rises slowly. "I'm honest, Alexa Jackson."

I love the way my name sounds as he pulls it from deep within him. The deep growl of his voice instantly touches my core. "We need to talk, Noah." I know that he's relaxed, happy and open and that's likely to change immediately once I bring up what happened the last time we saw each other in Boston.

"I know." He hangs his head down, his gaze falling to his knees. "I know we do."

Chapter 12

"The way you dumped me was brutal, Noah." I stretch my legs out and cross them. "It hurt so much."

"I was so fucked up that day." He pulls his right hand into a heavy fist. "I saw Brighton that morning and then Camilla and Abe showed up."

That's the opening I've been looking for. It's obvious, just from Noah's presence in New York, that there isn't an ongoing relationship between him and Camilla. I've sensed that all along. I took him at his word when he said that he was sending her to a hotel. "Have you seen Camilla?" It's vague but that's my intention. I want to know how invested in their lives he is. After seeing him and her in the same room almost naked together, my heart is still reeling. My mind's been convincing itself that there's nothing going on, but I need more reassurance. I need Noah to tell me directly and unequivocally that it's over for good.

"I sent the three of them away in a taxi after you left." He brushes his hand over my thigh. "I haven't seen Camilla or Abe since."

I'm relieved. I'm certain my expression shows it. That's one hurdle that I don't have to emotionally climb over anymore.

"She's back with her husband," he says with a small grin. "He's a glutton for punishment. I'm glad for Abe though."

"The baby is beautiful." It's a small offering but it's coming from an honest place. I'd thought about that baby more and more since Sadie had shared the news about her own pregnancy. Abe is an innocent participant in Camilla's manipulations. Even so, there was no mistaking the obvious love in her eyes when she was staring at him in that bedroom.

"He's a prince." His eyes study my face. "Tell me what to do to make this right, Alexa."

I pull my hands across my forehead, pushing the hair back from my face. "I've never really understood why you dumped me." I stop and think carefully before continuing, "I know it was overwhelming when we left the apartment. It's just that...that..."I stammer as I search for the right words. "It's just that you didn't want to listen to me at all. You just threw me out and then ignored me for weeks."

I see the pain ride over his expression as I throw the words at him. "You're right," he winces. "I was such a fucking asshole to you."

"I left Boston because I needed to get away from you." It's meant to hurt him. It's also true. A big part of the reason I left home was to escape all the memories of Noah that were clouding my mind. I also wanted to focus on my career and when the substitute teacher position came up it was a sign that my time in Boston was done.

"When I was stabbed," he takes a deep breath, holding his hand to his bare abdomen. The shiver that accompanies it races through him. "I was afraid to look in the mirror for weeks."

Although he's shared disjointed details of that night, he's never confided in me about how he felt. "I can't imagine how hard it must have been."

"When I finally did, I was disgusted by the way I looked." His hand jumps to the scar, his fingers tracing along it almost effortlessly. Anyone watching the motion would know that he's done it time and time again. He knows the landscape of his scarred face better than anyone. He's lived with it for years now. It's a constant reminder of the risk he took in loving Camilla. It's part of him now. It's unwanted, that's always been clear.

I want to reach out and touch him and tell him that I think it's beautiful. I want to reassure him that it's part of what drew me to him in the first place. I don't move. I can't break the rush of emotion that is pouring out of him. I won't. I need him to be open and vulnerable with me. This is how we move forward together.

"I used to be handsome." There's no disguising the disappointment woven into the words. "I used to walk in rooms and people would turn to look at me."

"I understand." The offering is small but it's filled with truth. I do understand. I understand that he sees only a marred face when he catches a glimpse of himself.

He reaches to cup my hand in his. "Now when I walk into a room, people stare at me for another reason."

I trace the lines of his palm with my index finger. I can hear the pain seeping out of him. I can see it in how he's holding his frame. His back is pushed back into the couch, his shoulders tense and unyielding. "You're so beautiful, Noah," I whisper it, not wanting to discount anything he's feeling. He doesn't see what I see when I look at him. I'm doubtful anyone does.

"When I look at you..." His finger catches my jaw and pulls my chin up so my eyes are aligned with his. "I see myself differently."

I stare at the scar, not caring that I'm being obvious or blatant. It's beautiful. It transverses the entire length of his face, but it's a part of the foundation of who he is to me. "When I first saw you," I sigh as I tap my index finger into his palm. "That day when I first came to your apartment I thought you were so gorgeous."

"You were staring at my dick." He raises his brow. "Don't even deny it."

"I was." My gaze darts over his body. "Then you pointed out the scar to me and it just made you that much more beautiful."

"How can it beautiful?" He's not throwing the words at me in anger or distaste. There's genuine curiosity there. He wants to understand what I see when I look at him.

I pull my hand from his to cup his cheek, covering the scar. "It's not about how it changes your face to me, Noah." My thumb moves across his bottom lip. "I didn't know you without it. You wouldn't be the same Noah Foster to me if you didn't have it."

"You're not ashamed of it?" he asks in barely more than a whisper. "You wouldn't be embarrassed to go out with me in the light of day where people can see it?"

"I will go anywhere with you at any moment." I pull his lips apart lightly with the pressure of my thumb. "I'm proud to be with you."

"I'm scared." I watch his lips as the words spill out. "I'm scared to be out there."

"I know." I pull his hands to the side as I crawl into his lap. "I'll take care of you, Noah. I'll take care of you."

Chapter 13

"We haven't made love since that first night." He reaches over to help me button my jacket closed. "You know that I want to."

I smile at the admission. "I know." I also know that he hasn't pushed me back into his bed because he understands that I'd resist. I was overwhelmed with desire the first night that I saw him in New York, but now that's tempered. I want more understanding before I share myself in any way. He can feel that. I see it in the tender way he touches me and kisses me.

"I'm not fucking this up again." He bows to run his lips across my cheek. "You're going to help me love you the right way."

The word leaps out from all the others with the grace of a freight train. It hits me full force and I take a step back. "We're going to help each other," I correct. "I'll help you learn to venture outside these walls and you'll help me understand your fascination with women who look just like me."

He stands back up, pulling his entire frame into a straight line. He's so tall. I have to bend my neck to look into his eyes. "I know that you think you look like Camilla…"

"I know that we look very much alike," I interrupt. It's still an ongoing issue with me. The moment I saw her it was as though a veil of confusion was lifted. "Every call girl you've ever requested is a blonde, right?"

"No." He grabs my shoulders. "It's never been about that, Alexa."

"About what?" I ask.

He takes a heavy step closer so there's little more than a hair's breadth of distance between us. He wraps his hands around me, pulling my cheek into his bare chest. "I wasn't looking for someone like Camilla when you walked in."

I rest my hands around his waist, circling my index fingers through the belt buckles. "You asked me to stay because I looked like her, Noah. I know that."

"Yes," he admits in a quiet whisper. "I did want you to stay initially because you looked like her."

I sigh before dropping my hands from him. I pull them into a tight fist on my chest, widening the distance between us. "I knew it."

"Alexa." His tone is firm and sharp. "Many women look alike. They may have the same hair color. The contours of their eyes resemble someone else's. I can see similarities in one woman's brow next to another..." His lips run over my hair. "There is no woman on earth who looks like you to me."

I know that he means the words and that they're coming from his heart. I also know that he sees me in a much different light than Camilla. "When I look at her, I see me."

He tugs my shoulders back and bows his head down so we're staring directly at one another. "You're so much more beautiful than her. Your heart is pure and kind."

"That may be true," I say it with the hope that it is. I've tried very hard the past few months to be a kinder, more caring person. I've tried to use my time in Paris as a compass to guide me towards a life that isn't just about me. I've tried. I can't say that I've succeeded yet. I still can't deny that we look very similar. "Camilla called it that afternoon when she said we could be twins."

"I can tell you this, Alexa." His index finger skims over my chin. "I never think of her when I look at you."

The words are meant to comfort me but they only aggravate that part of me that sees Camilla's face when I look in the mirror. "I don't know how to believe that Noah." I don't. I want to believe it. I have to believe it if we're ever going to move forward into a place where I feel I can truly tell him I love him.

"That afternoon when Ari brought Camilla and Abe over, it threw me into a tailspin." He closes his eyes briefly, the long lashes skimming against his skin. "Brighton had just left and he'd shown me all those pictures of you. You were so happy in all of them. Your smile was wide and your face lit up."

I nod. I can't deny what he's saying. Those days with Brighton in Paris were happy. I was enjoying myself until I realized he was an asshole who was cheating on his girlfriend behind her back.

"When I looked at Camilla holding Abe, I saw you." He stares at me, his eyes locked fiercely on mine. "It wasn't because you two have the same cheekbone structure, or because your eyes are the same color."

"What then?"

He lowers his head until his forehead is touching mine. "It was because I saw a woman with a child. I saw the tenderness between a mother and a newborn and I knew then that if you and I ever had a child, you'd lose that smile. I knew that you'd carry the burden of taking our son or daughter into the world because I couldn't."

He's just jumped years into the future within a single breath. My heart and mind can't catch up. "You thought about us having a baby?"

"When I saw Camilla that day, I felt absolutely nothing for her. Nothing." He enunciates the word, clearly saying it to alleviate any lingering doubt I may still have. "I felt everything for you. I saw a glimpse into what our future could be and I panicked."

I stare at him, unsure if he's telling me that he sincerely ended things because he was already fast forwarding our connection to a place where we were building a life together or if he is simply trying to appease all the guilt that I see skirting beneath his eyes every time I look at him. "You were so cold to me that day. You pushed me out when I first got there."

"I told you I was an asshole." His mouth thins into a straight line. "I wanted you to go so you could find a life that was normal. A guy that wasn't as fucked up as me."

"You know that I want you…" my voice stalls as I run my hands over the length of his chest, circling the tattoos. "I've never stopped wanting you."

Chapter 14

"You haven't said anything about him leaving that apartment," Kayla says as she exits the taxi after me. "Are you happy living that life?"

I'm not. When I was back in Boston, I had pushed Noah to get out. I had wanted him to embrace the part of my life that I had. When I invited him to my birthday party, I knew deep down that he wouldn't be able to do it. I could see the horror skirt over his eyes when I suggested it. When we went to the movies, he'd held his hand over his face until we were in the veiled darkness of the theatre. Only then had he relaxed enough to hold my hand and kiss me. We've never spoken about that night and how his hand shook within mine the entire time we sat there together.

"He hasn't changed since he got here, has he?" She motions towards a building down the street. "I mean has he even asked you out at all?"

"It's nice here." I survey all the tall buildings, soaking in the beauty of the architecture in this part of the city. This is my first visit to Wall Street and I'm already in love with what it has to offer visually. "No," I say under my breath.

"He's not going to change, Lex." She pulls open the heavy glass door of what I assume is her office tower. "You have to decide if being in there with him is enough for you."

It is. At least I think it is. "I know," I offer back. "I know."

"Alexa." I feel a strong hand grab my shoulder before the husky voice of a man assaults me from behind. I feel his breath on my exposed neck and his grip tightens. My eyes dart to Kayla whose gaze is transfixed on whoever is standing directly behind me.

I spin around on my heel. His face is different in the light of day. The handsome sculpted features are accentuated by the hint of the five o'clock shadow that is misplaced this early in the morning. His green eyes soak in my frame, stopping to rest on the hint of cleavage that is peeking over the top of the neckline of my grey dress. "Alec," I say his name with little emotion. I haven't thought about him since that night at Axel NY when I'd bolted out of the restaurant in search of Noah.

"Who is this, Lex?" Kayla is standing so close to me now that anyone staring at us would be hard pressed to find where I end and she begins. I can feel her hand on my lower back. She's pushing into me, a sure sign that she wants a formal introduction.

"This is Alec." I stop there, realizing that we've never shared surnames. "Alec and I met at the restaurant."

Kayla slaps me hard across my lower back. I throw her a pained look before realizing that she's looking for an introduction. Since when is she so coy that she needs me to introduce her to any man?

"I'm Kayla," she says after reading between the lines of the scowl on my face. "Do you work here?"

A ghost of a smile skirts over his lips. "You could say that." He doesn't acknowledge Kayla. His eyes are fixed on me. "Are you looking for a third job, Alexa?"

He's trying to be funny but I'm not in the mood for harmless banter or flirting of any kind. I came here with the sole intention of watching Kayla give a presentation to a group of high school kids on a work assignment day. I'm here for one reason and one reason only and that's to support her. "I'm not," I snap. I'm being rude. I can feel it. I don't mean to be. I want to be cordial, sweet and nice but I'm lost in thoughts of Noah stuck in his apartment and what that really may mean for my future.

"That's unfortunate." His eyes skim me one more time before he glances at his wristwatch. "I'm late for a meeting."

"I work on the tenth floor," Kayla blurts out shamelessly. "I'm here every day." She may as well stick a sign that reads 'horny and available' to her head.

"Can I call you, Alexa?" He reaches for my hand but I instinctively pull it back. I don't want to give off any signals that aren't loud and clear. I'm not interested. He's handsome, he's charming and he's got a sexual pull that is unmistakable.

"I'm involved with someone now."

"My loss." He tips his head before leaning back on his heel. "If that changes, you have my number."

Arrogant and hot. No wonder Kayla is practically drooling all over my shoulder in an effort to get him to notice her.

We both watch in silence as he walks towards the glass doors, a burly man opens one for him as Alec walks through and into the pedestrian traffic in front of the building.

"Holy hell that guy was smoking hot," Kayla whispers into my ear. "That's the guy you wore the blue dress for?"

"That's the guy." I nod.

"A guy like that, Lex…that kind of a guy, he doesn't hide away from anything." Her voice is breathy, the tone high. "That's the kind of guy that takes you out just so he can watch other men stare at you before he takes you home and fucks you for hours."

She's right. That's exactly what Alec's demeanor screams and it's the exact opposite of who Noah Foster is.

Chapter 15

"I'm doing some substitute work for a school in Brooklyn this week." I twirl the spaghetti Noah ordered in around on the fork. "They have an afterschool program that I've been helping with too."

"That sounds great." He pulls a napkin over his lips as he finishes the last bite on his plate. "This was delicious. How'd you hear about this place?"

"My friend went on a date there," I wince as the words leave my lips. "I mean she tried the food there and loved it." Kayla had actually raved last night about not only the food at the small Italian place two blocks from Noah's apartment, but at the guy she went there with. They're going out again tonight. This time to a club.

"It bothers you, doesn't it?" He's never been one to avoid any subject. When Noah wants to talk about something, he dives in, naked and exposed. Speaking of which, he hasn't had a stitch of clothing on since I arrived. I even had to push him into the hallway when the delivery guy got here. Suddenly, it's feeling as though we're moving backwards instead of forward.

"Of course." It's a response meant to pull at his curiosity. He already knows that I would have preferred to have gone to the restaurant. I hadn't suggested it because he'd look uncomfortable and tell me that he didn't feel up to it. It's the same dance steps we'd perfected back in Boston. He isn't making any effort to move outside of this cocoon either.

He stands and my eyes instantly hone in on his cock. It's beautiful, but it's a wicked reminder of the reason why he pushed me away in the first place. If I nag him about wanting to go out I'm fearful that he'll push harder this time and any promise of a future together that we might have had will be gone for good. I can't keep wishing things were different though. I can't keep carrying around the senseless hope that one day he'll decide that the world outside his sheltered hiding space is not going to emotionally destroy him.

"I hate being stared at." I'm not sure if the words are directed at me personally or if he's speaking in generalities.

"I was only staring at your dick." I motion towards it with my fork. My appetite has escaped me. "I thought you were going to wear pants more often."

"I was hot." He winks before he picks up both of our dinner plates and pads off down the hallway towards the kitchen.

I'm frustrated. Not just because he consistently makes light of everything dark, mysterious and closed off about him, but also because I feel as though he's never going to venture outside of the world he's built for himself. We were making progress in Boston until Brighton showed him those pictures and Camilla gave him a glimpse into what his world would be with a baby.

"Tell me about the school." He's back, nodding towards the large couch in the next room.

I follow silently hoping that I'll somehow find the strength within the few steps from here to there to bring up the subject that is almost leaping off my tongue.

"Do you like it there?" His words feel misplaced and I can't mentally push myself back to where we were just a few minutes ago.

"Where?" I ask softly as I settle in next to him on the large sofa. I pull my sweater tighter around my frame. I need a barrier between my body and his.

"The school, Alexa… the one in Brooklyn? How's that going?"

I smile softly remembering how exhilarating today had been. I'm in charge of an entire class of nine-year-olds and although it was intimidating two days ago when I started the assignment, I'm finding my groove now. I belong in the classroom and this random substitute teacher work is proving that to me more and more every time I step foot into a new school. "I love it," I admit. "The children are amazing. I stayed late because they have an afterschool program."

"You're beaming." His finger jumps to my chin. "You're so happy."

Guilt rushes through me at the word. It's the same word he used back in Boston when he unceremoniously kicked me to the curb. I curse inwardly, knowing that it might just bring up all those repressed feelings that he's been ignoring since he arrived in Manhattan. Sooner or later my happiness is going to chase the man of my dreams into the corner again and I'm going to have to face that.

"Noah," I pause as I search for the words. I'm not one to give up easily so I'm going to ask one more time. I need to give him a chance to prove that he wants more than what exists here. I can't be the only contact he has with the outside world. I can't just continue to be the light in all of his darkness. It's going to suffocate me. I'm going to miss my chance to enjoy all that my life could be offering me because I'm terrified that my joy will send him reeling. "The afterschool program is having a series of workshops and I was wondering something."

His tall body tenses immediately. I watch his shoulders pull back from me with a seamless grace that no one else would notice. It's effortless and subtle but it's telling. It means he's steeling himself for the question I'm about to ask. He knows I'm going to push for something he isn't comfortable with. "What's that?"

"They're looking for a photographer to lead one session with some of the children." I stop to look at his face but his gaze is cast down. He's grazing his hand along his thigh. The motion is unreadable.

"They wouldn't want me, Alexa."

"Why not?" I push back. "I've already asked if you could do it."

"You what?" He bolts to his feet in one swift movement. "You did that without asking me first?"

The veiled anger in his voice is tempered. I've never seen him pushed to the limits of rage. I've only seen small glimpses of what brews beneath the surface.

"I was just inquiring," I say softly. "I know that some schools don't want to associate with a photographer who takes nude photos. They are fine with it."

"You had no right doing that."

It bites. It may be true but it bites. "I did it because these children don't have anything and the idea of working with a photographer like you would be a gift to them."

"I'm not doing it." He brushes against the coffee table, causing it to move slightly. "Don't ever volunteer me for anything again without asking me."

"I won't." I stand now too. "I'm going home. I have a very long day tomorrow." I want to push back and insult him for not taking the kids into consideration. I want to tell him to get over himself already and accept that he's scarred. I want to tell him to let it go but I can't. All I can do is give in to the desire to get into bed and fall asleep.

"You're working at the school again tomorrow?" He's not asking out of curiosity. The question is meant to fill the empty gap of silence between us.

"There and the restaurant." I nudge him with my elbow, wanting him to move out of my way.

"When will you come over again?"

"I've busy for the next few days," I lie. I need time to decompress and think about what I'm doing. Can I really be satisfied being in a relationship with him? I'm in love with him but his life is so different than mine. I can't keep ignoring that. I won't keep ignoring it.

"Text me when you can come back." He brushes his lips against my forehead. "I'll be waiting."

I touch his cheek softly and rest my face against his strong chest for a moment before I head out the door.

Chapter 16

"You're serious?" He pulls his lips together in a grimace. "You seriously don't remember me?"

Who in their right mind would have imagined that I'd get hit on so much in an upscale restaurant in New York City? I am getting more action here than I had the entire time I worked at Star Bistro in Boston. The café had been milling with college aged men and I was lucky if I ever got a second look there. Here, I can't even deliver an entrée of grilled lamb to the table five feet away because this guy won't get the hell out of my way.

"Look at my face again." He touches his strong jaw. "You've got to remember. It's Alexa, right?"

The fact that he knows my name irks me. He's like a slightly taller version of Alec. This one has black hair, striking blue eyes and a drop dead gorgeous face. "I don't."

"We met years ago in Boston." He taps his finger along his bottom lip. "You look exactly the same now as you did then."

I nod. My eyes flit past him to where the couple who ordered the lamb is sitting in the corner. They haven't glanced at me but I need to bring their food to the table before it gets cold. "I'm really busy, sir."

"Sir?" The word grumbles out from between his full lips. "You weren't calling me that back then."

This game of whatever the fuck this guy is playing is annoying. I just want him to move over so I can get back to work. "I don't know who you are. I'm sorry. If we met, I apologize for that, but I'm juggling a full table load tonight."

"My name is Nathan."

"Nathan?" I scan his face. "I don't know a Nathan."

"You've never met a man named Nathan?" There's no denying that he's unimpressed with that answer.

"Did you come into Star Bistro when I worked there?" I ask sweetly. That's probably how he knows my name. Maybe he has one of those photographic memories that captures snippets from the past and files them away in some corner of his brain.

"We fucked."

I feel the color drain from my face the moment I lock eyes with him. "You and I fucked?"

"We met at a club there." He leans a touch forward. "We went up to my suite."

I stare at his face, ignoring the words he's saying. "You're him?"

"Don't look so surprised," he says jokingly. "I thought I was more memorable than that."

"You look nothing like I remember." I clench my jaw. This is the guy that I couldn't stop thinking about for years? There's no denying he's hot but why can't I place his face? Why did I hold onto that memory so long when the details were obviously so misplaced?

"It hasn't been that long," he stresses the word 'that', making a clear point that we slept together only four years ago. Why does it suddenly feel like a different lifetime ago? Why did I make such a big deal over him when I can't even remember his face?

"Why are you here?" I search the area behind him, my eyes locked on the couple sitting in silence. She's studying the menu while he reads the paper. They're so disconnected. I've watched them for a few minutes and they haven't said one word to each other.

"I'm dating one of the sous chefs." He bolts his head to the side to get within my scope of vision. "Jessica."

"Jessica is a sweetheart." I lock eyes with him briefly. "You're lucky to have her."

"I am." I can hear the confusion in his voice. "You're sure you don't remember me?"

"I thought I did," I confess. "I remember we had a lot of fun." I blush as the words leave my lips. Fun? This is the guy that fucked me for hours and I call that fun? Why does it mean so much less now than when Noah asked me about him just a few months ago?

"I'm glad I ran into you, Alexa." The expression on his face doesn't match the words. "You've helped me with something."

"I've helped you," I chuckle. "With what?"

"With realizing how lucky I am to have Jessica." His face shifts slightly at the mention of her name. "I love her a lot."

"I'm glad." My eyes bolt to the bank of windows at the front of the restaurant. There's a man wearing a hoodie covering his head peering through the glass. His face is memorable. I'll never forget it. Forty years from now I'll still recall each and every detail of every part of him. He smiles slightly as his eyes lock with mine. "I need to go. My life is waiting for me."

Chapter 17

"Who was that guy?" Noah looks down at me. "That looked intense."

I shrug my shoulders. "That was Nathan."

"The Nathan." He pulls air quotes around the two words. "The best sex you've ever had Nathan."

"Apparently," I say quietly. "I didn't recognize him at all." I'm still reeling from that. What does it say about me? Have I fucked so many men that I've lost track of what they look like?

"You didn't?" He can't hide the grin that's pulling at the corner of his mouth.

"Forget him," I say flippantly.

"I will," he tosses back. "You already have."

I smile softly. "I have. What are you doing here?"

"I wanted to see you." He fidgets from one foot to the next. The worn sneakers he's wearing gliding across the pavement of the crowded sidewalk. "I just wanted to see your face."

I smile at the confession. I reach for his hand. "I have to work a few more hours."

"I can't come inside, Alexa." He motions towards the crowded restaurant. "I can sit out here on that bench for a while."

I glance down at the wooden bench a few feet from the entrance to Axel. "Will you wait for me?"

"Forever." He reaches down to kiss me gently on my lips. "I like that you forgot him."

"Who?"

His lips curve into a wide smile. "Everyone but me."

***

"Will you stay with me tonight?" He loops my arm around his before resting his hand over mine.

I snuggle my palm into the soft fabric of the hoodie he's wearing. Paired with dark colored sweat pants he looks imposing and dangerous. People passing us don't gaze at him and I know it only adds to his apprehension about the scar. It's the reason he has the hood pulled up around his head.

"I can have a driver take you to school in the morning."

I glance down at my white blouse and black skirt. "I can't go to school dressed like this. I'll leave a little early to go to my place so I can shower and dress."

"You'll stay then?"

"Yes." I nod. "Are we walking all the way there?" My feet are killing me. I've been on them the entire day and normally I'd go home and soak in a long, hot bath.

"I can call a driver." He reaches into the pocket of the hoodie pulling out his smartphone.

"I'll just hail a taxi." I dart from his side and head for the curb. His arms are around me in an instant.

"No." He almost shouts the word into the darkened air. "I don't like taxis. I'll get a driver."

I stand in stunned silence, watching taxi after taxi whiz past us as he punches at the screen of his smartphone calling a driver to come get us.

***

"I'm getting in with you. Move over."

I push my ass along the bottom of the large bathtub hoping that I've made enough room for Noah to climb in. He bends each of his long legs, elegantly lowering himself into the warm water behind me.

"This is heaven." He pulls my back into his muscular chest, his hands lazily running over my exposed breasts. We haven't been intimate since that first night when I discovered him here, in New York.

"It feels so nice, Noah." I reach to cradle his hands in mine. "I love being close to you."

"I could stay here with you forever, Alexa," he says naturally and smoothly.

It opens a door for me that I know he wants kept closed. When I saw him on the street tonight, hiding himself beneath the heavy clothing he was wearing it hit me how vulnerable he really is. That, combined with my awkward encounter with Nathan, have convinced me that I am going to overcome every obstacle that Noah and I have. I need to. I can't let him go.

"Do you want me to wash your back?" He reaches for a bar of scented soap sitting on the edge of the porcelain tub. "Scoot forward a bit."

I do as I'm told and a soft moan leaves my body as his hands glide smoothly over my back. "That feels amazing, Noah."

"You feel amazing." His hands move along my back before sliding across my chest. He cups both my breasts in his hands, his fingers pinching my now hardening nipples.

I reach back to try and circle his cock with my hand but he pushes against me. "Please, Noah."

"Let me have this," he growls in my ear. "Let me make you come."

I slide back until I'm leaning into his chest. His hands dart down. His fingers slide across my wetness, opening my folds.

"You're so perfect." His words are barely audible.

"I want to come," I say breathlessly. It's felt like years since his hands were on my body. I'm wet. Even in the stillness of the water I can feel how wet I am just by the slightest touch of his fingers on my flesh.

He rubs his index finger in slow circles over my clit, building everything into a fevered pitch within me. His other hand traces a path back to my breasts, twisting my nipple. "Come for me, Alexa. Come for me."

I race to the edge. My body naturally falling back into him as his lips glide over my neck before his teeth bite down into my shoulder. I call out his name from within a moan just as I feel him buck his hips. His warm desire hits the bottom of my back as he finds his own release.

Chapter 18

"I'm so good in bed...or in the bath," I correct myself. "I'm so good that I didn't even have to touch you and you came."

He blushes slightly at the words. "The sounds you were making were so fucking hot."

I raise my hips so he can pull the blanket down. "It feels incredible when you touch me there."

"There?" He cocks a brow. "On your pussy, you mean?"

I scratch the side of my nose. "Yes, there."

"When the hell did you get so shy?" He pulls back the sheet to reveal my naked body. "Are you the same girl who stripped naked for me right after we met?"

"I didn't love you then." I stop. My eyes fill with tears. I said it. Not the way I wanted to. It's not the romantic scenario that I envisioned but the words are out there now. He knows it.

"You love me, Alexa." There's no hint of a question there. He's not asking me anything. He's simply stating the obvious.

I pat the bed next to me, wanting him beside me. He quickly acquiesces. "When did you know?"

I can't say the words again right now. I need for them to settle in the air between us before I do that.

"When you came to get me to take me to New York."

"You knew then?"

"When we were in my office." He pulls his hand around my waist, his cock settling next to my thigh. "I knew then that you were in love with me."

I was. I hadn't been able to admit it to him or myself, but he's right. I did love him then. "How did you know?"

"You wanted to fight for me." His voice cracks slightly before he regains complete control. "You wanted to give me a life outside of my apartment."

I pull my head down to the sheet, hoping to ward off all the conflicting emotions that are rushing through me. "I still want that."

"It's hard for me."

"I know." I do know. I know that he's scared of what people will think when they see the scar. I know venturing out to Axel NY tonight was a huge step for him. I know that if I push this too much, he's going to pull back so hard that I'll feel alone and miserable again.

"Alexa." His hand cups my jaw. "I need to tell you something."

"What?" I study his expression trying to find anything that might indicate what he's about to confess. "Is it about Ari?"

"Ari?" Her name sounds as distasteful coming from his lips as it does in my own mind. I haven't thought about her since he's been in New York. He hasn't mentioned her at all, which seems misplaced given the fact that he's confessed in the past that they're close friends.

"It's stupid, but there's something…" I stall. "I wanted to ask you about the woman that Bernie saw at your apartment."

"When?" His eyes scan my face. "When did Bernie see a woman there?"

"You called the restaurant there a few weeks ago and asked for me to bring you a sandwich and then Bernie did and he told Hunter there was a woman there." Christ, that sounds as stupid coming out of me as it has when it's been bouncing through my random thoughts for weeks.

"That was Ari." Again with the no-holds-barred answers. "She was there picking up some shit she left there."

"What kind of shit?"

"Magazines, some picture she gave me that she took of herself. I kept it in a drawer because her selfies shouldn't see the light of day." He cocks a brow along with a grin. "She was leaving town and wanted her stuff so I told her to come get it."

"She left town?"

"Weeks ago." He shrugs his shoulders. "She hooked up with some guy and they took off for California. I haven't heard from her since."

I don't know where the wash of relief that flows over me comes from, but it's welcomed. "I'm glad."

"You're glad?" He jokes. "I'm fucking over the moon ecstatic."

I laugh gently. "That's not what you wanted to tell me, is it?"

"No." His expression immediately shifts from carefree to stoic. "It's not about Ari."

"It's not about Brighton, is it?"

"Brighton went back to Paris days ago." Noah brushes his fingers through my hair. "He's giving it another shot with Liz. He was here visiting his newborn nephew."

I feel even more relieved now knowing that Brighton isn't going to pop up without warning to derail everything. "Good."

"Can I talk now?" he asks. "I want you to understand something. It's something I've never told anyone."

I can feel the seriousness of his words bore into me. "Tell me, Noah. Tell me." I roll to my side so I'm facing him directly.

"Alexa." He reaches for my hand, pulling it into his. My lips skirt over my palm. "I hate my scar."

I nod. "I know." I pull my hand from his to cradle his cheek. I run my index finger over the jagged edge of the scar.

"You don't know why." He pulls his brows together before his lip quivers. "I've never told anyone the reason why."

"You said because it changed how you looked," I offer. That was what he told me. It's been the reason why he hasn't wanted to face the world.

"No." He shakes his head softly. My hand follows the movement, never losing contact with his face. "It's more."

"What?"

"It reminds me of what I did." He bites his bottom lip, pulling strength from the pain. "I should have gone to prison for what I did."

"No." I lean forward quickly brushing my lips against his. "No, Noah. You did it to protect yourself and Camilla."

"I took a man's life." His body jerks forward with a sob. "I stole his life from him."

I can't hold back the tears. Watching this beautiful, strong, resilient man break down is tearing at my own heart. "You had to."

"I could have handled it differently." His voice changes pitch as he struggles to hold in his emotions. "I should have done something else."

"Noah." I bolt to my knees now before I pull my body over his. "You couldn't have done anything differently."

"Alexa." He looks into my eyes. His brown eyes are clouded with a mask of tears. "I shouldn't have a life either. I took his, I don't deserve a life."

I stare at his face. I can't take my eyes off the scar that has come to define the person he is. I suddenly see the mask of darkness fade away. The light that has been missing beneath his gaze is trickling through. "You deserve a beautiful, happy life with me."

"I want that, Alexa." He nods through his tears. "I want to let go and live with you."

"He would have killed you both, Noah," I say it with true conviction. "He would have taken your life and hers. Don't let him steal the rest of your life now."

"I'm scared." He clings to my waist. "I'm scared of being happy."

"Let me show you how, Noah." I rest my lips against his. "Please let me show you how."

"I will." He pulls me into his arms. "I promise I will. Never let me go, Alexa."

"Never, Noah." I wrap myself tightly around him. "Never in a million years."

Epilogue

Six Months Later

"I would have given you that ring months ago if I would have known you'd stare at it endlessly," he growls into my ear. "I love seeing you smile like that."

I don't think I've stopped smiling since Noah proposed last night. I've hoped for months that he would ask me to be his wife. Now that it's happening I can't focus on anything, let alone the lesson plan I'm supposed to be preparing for tomorrow.

"Do you want me to come by after school again?" He kneels down next to where I'm sitting by the desk in our office. "I picked up some photography books today that I want to share with the kids."

"They'll love that, Noah." I graze my lips softly over his. "They love everything you bring to them."

"I love everything they give to me." He taps his hand across his naked chest. "It's good practice for when we have a baby."

"Noah." I pat my hand against his cheek. "I told you that I wanted to wait until after the wedding." I lift my hand in the air, allowing the light on the desk to catch the diamond's glare. "It's huge though. Why did you get me such a big ring?"

"It's as big as my love for you." He pulls his hands together in front of his chest. "You like when I'm romantic."

"I like when you're happy," I correct him. "Do you have any shoots tomorrow?"

He pulls his smartphone from the pocket of his jeans. "I have a newborn baby at ten in the morning in Chelsea but that's negotiable. It's all about his schedule. Then I have four-year-old twins in Soho at one. They should have had lunch by then so hopefully they'll cooperate."

"They'll be thrilled when you show up with that suitcase of toys you cart around with you." I nod towards the camera equipment that Noah has stored in the corner of his office. It's a constant reminder of his new business, photographing children. Settling into his father's place together had worked out beautifully after Kayla decided to leave New York to go back to Boston. Her old high school boyfriend had suddenly declared his undying love for her and her heart took her right back to his doorstep and his arms. When I talked to her yesterday, she sounded giddy.

"It's a bag of tricks, Alexa." He playfully teases me. "What time are Sadie and her kids coming on Saturday?"

I love the effortless ease that floats in the air between us now. He's an integral part of my life and I've woven myself into his in much the same way. We share everything now and his love of Sadie's stepson Cory and her new baby daughter, Olivia, is unmistakable. He cares for Sadie just as much as I do. The time we've spent with her in Boston after the arrival of baby Olivia has transformed our bond. We both know, without question, that we'll have a family together. We know that our destiny is each other.

"They're flying here." I run my thumb over my smart phone. "Their flight arrives at ten in the morning at JFK. I'd really like…"

"You'd really like if we could go to pick them up at the airport?" He finishes my sentence.

"I'd really like if you fucked me right now." I slam the cover over my tablet. "I'd like if you showed me just how badly you want to marry me."

"You want me as badly right now as you did that day you brought me a sandwich back in Boston." He scoops me up in his arms in one easy movement.

"No. You wanted me then. I just wanted my tip." I slide my arms around his neck. "I couldn't believe that I'd landed in the apartment of the Noah Foster."

"Christ, I was an arrogant son-of-a-bitch then." He lays me softly down on the blanket on our bed. "I remember you couldn't take your eyes off my dick."

I pull myself up so I'm resting on my elbows. "That's because you had it on display. You knew I'd fall for you when you opened the door."

He pushes his jeans down releasing his beautiful cock. "I fell for you, Alexa. So hard, so fast and so completely." His hands work quickly to undo the belt on my dress.

"I'm still falling for you." I reach to help him, ridding myself of the dress, panties and bra. "I'll never stop. I love you so much."

He crawls over me, pushing my hands above my head and into the soft fabric. "You're my everything, Alexa. My everything."

Thank You!

Thank you for purchasing and downloading my book. I can't even begin to put to words what it means to me. If you enjoyed it, please remember to write a review for it. Let me know your thoughts! I want to keep my readers happy.

I have more exciting books on the way, such as standalone novels and more serials, so stay tuned to my website, www.deborahbladon.com. There are interactive forums and other goodies to check out, plus all of my book trailers!

If you want to chat with me personally, please LIKE my page on Facebook. I love connecting with all of my readers because without you, none of this would be possible. www.facebook.com/authordeborahbladon

Thank you, for everything. xo

About the Author

Deborah Bladon has never read a romance hero she didn't like. Her love for romance novels began when she was old enough to board the bus, library card in hand to check out the newest Harlequin paperbacks. She's a Canadian by heart, and by passport, but you can often spot her in New York City sipping a latte and looking for inspiration for her next story. Manhattan is definitely her second home.

She cherishes her family and believes that each day is a gift for writing, for reading, and for loving.

Printed in Great Britain
by Amazon.co.uk, Ltd.,
Marston Gate.